"Do you remember what I said I would do if you called me Mr. Cazorra?" he drawled.

Diego's silver wolf's eyes gleamed with a feral hunger as he drew Clare's face down to his and angled his mouth over her lips. His kiss was like no other she had ever experienced, deeply sensual and so utterly irresistible that she did not stand a chance against his skillful seduction.

Still half-dazed with sleep, but more dazzled by him, her lips parted of their own volition when his mouth exerted subtle pressure. Like a connoisseur of fine wine, he tasted her slowly and unhurriedly yet with such bone-shaking eroticism that she melted against him.

The sense of unreality she had felt since she'd arrived in Brazil increased, and she sank into a dreamlike state where she was only conscious of the strength of Diego's arms around her and the divine smell of him, the taste of him when she dipped her tongue into his mouth. He overwhelmed her, and the feel of his hand smoothing up and down her spine evoked a languorous warmth in her veins.

He deepened the kiss, and the languorous feeling was replaced with a fierce pull of desire in the pit of her stomach so that she lifted her hips, unconsciously seeking to assuage the ache inside her. She sensed a new urgency in Diego, a barely controlled savagery as he ravished her mouth with his intoxicating mastery, taking everything she offered him and demanding more.

Bought by the Brazilian

Claimed by passion!

Cruz Delgado and Diego Cazorra—two men brought up in Brazil's favelas—have literally dragged themselves up from dirt to a diamond empire.

But having the world at their feet and dripping with their jewels is not enough. Now they will have their revenge against the women who walked away.

It's time for Cruz and Diego to claim what's theirs... and for both of these women to be *Bought by the Brazilian*!

Read Cruz and Sabrina's story:

Mistress of His Revenge

Read Diego and Clare's story in:

Master of Her Innocence

Chantelle Shaw

MASTER OF HER
INNOCENCE

HARLEQUIN PRESENTS®

Recycling programs
for this product may
not exist in your area.

ISBN-13: 978-0-373-13453-3

Master of Her Innocence

First North American Publication 2016

Copyright © 2016 by Chantelle Shaw

Printed in U.S.A.

Chantelle Shaw lives on the Kent coast and thinks up her stories while walking on the beach. She has been married for over thirty years and has six children. Her love affair with reading and writing Harlequin stories began as a teenager, and her first book was published in 2006. She likes strong-willed, slightly unusual characters. Chantelle also loves gardening, walking and wine!

Books by Chantelle Shaw

Visit the Author Profile page at Harlequin.com for more titles.

For *New York Times* bestselling historical romance author Sarah MacLean, who gave brilliant workshops at RWA 2015 and inspired me to go with my crazy ideas and write bonkers! Thank you, Sarah.

CHAPTER ONE

'SISTER ANN, DO I really need to wear a habit?' Clare Marchant looked doubtfully at the Mother Superior. 'It seems wrong to pretend that I belong to the Holy Order of the Sacred Heart. I feel like I am an imposter.'

'My child, I strongly advise that for your safety you should dress as a nun. Torrente is one of the most dangerous places in Brazil. Its close proximity to the border with Colombia has made it a route for drug smuggling and people trafficking and I have heard of young women in the town who have been forced into prostitution. It is a lawless place where even the police are too scared to visit. The men who run the drugs cartels have little respect for life, but they do at least retain some respect for the church.'

The Mother Superior smiled gently at Clare, noting the signs of strain on the young Englishwoman's face and the shadows beneath her eyes that told of too many sleepless nights of worry.

'There is no need for you to feel like an imposter.

You have come to Brazil with the selfless intention to search for your sister and pay the ransom her kidnappers have demanded. You are bravely prepared to put yourself in danger to help someone you love, and at least the church can offer you some small measure of protection.' Sister Ann's expression became grave. 'I'm sure I don't have to remind you that the men who took Becky are utterly ruthless.'

Clare followed the nun's gaze to what looked like a jewellery box on the desk, and a feeling of nausea swept over her as she pictured the gruesome contents of the casket. *Don't think of it*, she ordered herself. But her mind visualised the severed tip of an earlobe wrapped in layers of tissue paper like some ghastly mimicry of a gift from a lover. Surely it wasn't a piece of Becky's ear? She could not bear to think of her beautiful sister being mutilated by whoever had snatched her from the street outside the five-star hotel in Rio de Janeiro where Becky had been modelling for a photo shoot.

She tore her eyes from the box and stared at what she could see of her reflection in the small mirror hanging on the wall of the Mother Superior's office. The grey habit Sister Ann had lent her fell to just above her ankles to reveal a pair of flat black lace-up shoes. She watched the Sister place a veil on her head. With her auburn hair covered up she looked different—more elegant and sophisticated like Becky—although the sprinkling of freckles on her nose were a giveaway clue to her vibrant mane hidden beneath the veil, she thought ruefully.

'If it helps your conscience, I have given you a white veil; they are worn by novice nuns before they take their final vows when they change to a black veil,' Sister Ann explained. 'That way, it is not entirely untruthful for you to appear to be a young woman who is contemplating a religious life. And, after all, you were drawn to seek comfort at the chapel of Santa Maria when you arrived in Rio de Janeiro. Many of us are called to our vocation in mysterious ways.'

Clare could not bring herself to admit to the kindly nun that she did not believe her future was to follow a life of religious devotion. Although the fact that she was still a virgin at the age of twenty-four meant that she fitted the requirement of chastity, she thought wryly. Mark had called her a prude, but she didn't think she was. She had simply wanted to be sure he was the right man for her, and it turned out that he hadn't been.

England and her break-up with Mark seemed a million miles away, and she wondered if she would wake up to find that her sister being kidnapped was a bad dream rather than a living nightmare. But, unbelievable though it was, the situation was real. On Monday morning she had arrived for work as usual at her parents' company, A-Star PR, and received a frantic phone call from her father with the astonishing news that her younger sister Becky, an internationally famous model, had been kidnapped.

'The kidnappers have sent a letter saying they will kill Becky unless I follow their instructions.' Rory Marchant had sounded shaken. 'They want me to go to Brazil and pay a ransom, but I can't leave your mother, and I daren't tell her that Becky's life is in danger. The specialist said it is important that Tammi doesn't suffer any kind of stress. She was lucky to survive the first stroke, and a second one could kill her.' Rory had broken down. 'Clare, I don't know what to do. I want to rescue my precious girl, but I don't want to lose my wife.'

'I'll go to Brazil and take the ransom money to the kidnappers,' Clare had said instantly. 'You can't leave Mum, especially now that she is finally showing signs of recovering.'

She had dismissed the little voice in her head, which whispered that her father had never thought of her as his precious girl. It had always been her sister who had come first in their parents' affections, but it was unsurprising after Becky had been seriously ill and nearly died when she was a child, Clare reminded herself. She loved Becky and could only imagine how terrified her sister must be feeling right now.

She blinked back a sudden rush of tears and turned to the Mother Superior. 'Thank you for helping me. All the Sisters have been so kind. I felt scared and alone when Sister Carmelita spoke to me in the chapel in Rio.'

Clare's thoughts flew back to two days ago when she had arrived in Rio de Janeiro and, following the kidnappers' instructions, had checked into a run-down motel to wait for the gang to contact her. But, instead of receiving a letter telling her what to do next, as had happened when the kidnappers had contacted her father in England, this time she had been sent a package, and when she had opened it and seen the grisly, severed piece of earlobe, she had rushed to the bathroom to be sick.

The note sent with the box had instructed her to go to the town of Torrente, which she had found on a map was in the far west of Brazil, over two thousand miles from Rio and deep in the Amazon rainforest. It had been at that point, exhausted and fearful that the kidnappers had hurt her sister, that she had been inexplicably drawn to step inside the church near her motel, and she had broken down and told the nun she had met about Becky being kidnapped. Within twenty-four hours Sister Carmelita had arranged for Clare to catch an internal flight to the city of Manaus in northern Brazil, and she had been staying with the nuns of the Holy Order of the Sacred Heart while Sister Ann arranged her onward journey to Torrente.

'I wish you would reconsider your decision to try to rescue your sister alone and go to the police.'

'I *can't*. The kidnappers said they would kill Becky if I told anyone they are holding her. I'm scared I may have put her life in danger by accepting help from the Sisters—' Clare's voice trembled '—but I didn't know what else to do.'

'I am afraid the kidnapping of wealthy tourists is becoming a growing problem in Brazil, and it is sadly true that often the police are unable to track down the kidnap gangs,' the Mother Superior said heavily. The sound of a vehicle driving into the courtyard drew her to the window. 'Mr Cazorra is here and, God willing, you will soon be reunited with your sister.'

Clare picked up the rucksack she had packed with a few of her own clothes and other essentials. 'The gold prospector you have asked to take me to Torrente doesn't know why I'm going, does he?'

'Don't worry, your secret will remain within the walls of the convent. I have explained to Diego that you are to take up a post teaching at the Sunday school and you must reach the town by the weekend.'

Fear cramped in Clare's stomach. Sunday was when the kidnappers had said they would contact her again to tell her where she should take the ransom money. She picked up the leather briefcase that held five hundred thousand pounds in used bank notes. It was a terrifying thought that Becky's very life was contained in the briefcase and Clare gripped the handle tightly.

'I should warn you about the gold prospector,' Sister Ann said.

'Warn me?' Clare's tension ratcheted up a notch. 'You said I could trust him.'

'I don't doubt he will get you to Torrente safely. He knows that area of the Amazon rainforest better than anyone I can think of. Mr Cazorra is a good man who has helped the Sisters in the past, but he has a reputation for...' The nun paused before saying delicately, 'Well, let's just say that he enjoys the company of women. Many women. He is very charming.'

'You mean he's a flirt?' Were all Brazilian men Lotharios? Clare wondered, remembering the taxi driver who had driven her from Manaus Airport to the convent. The man had greasy hair and was wearing a sweat-stained T-shirt, but he had suggested that he would give her a free tour of the city if she went to bed with him. Needless to say, she had declined his invitation.

All she could think about was saving her sister and the news that her escort to Torrente was a womaniser was the least of her concerns. 'I'm sure I'll be able to handle your Mr Cazorra,' she said grimly as she followed the Mother Superior outside to the courtyard.

Diego Cazorra glanced up at the stained-glass window of the convent and noticed how the sunlight shining through the coloured glass reflected a rainbow effect on to the floor of the courtyard. It was strange how beauty was often found in the simplest things, he mused. At the diamond mine he owned with his close friend and business partner Cruz Delgado, he had discovered some of the most fabulous diamonds ever found in Brazil. But the purity of sunlight touched his soul in a way that glittering gemstones never could.

The two years he had spent in one of Brazil's most notoriously violent jails had taught him to appreciate the simple things in life: the feel of warm sunshine on his face every time he came up from a mineshaft, or the sight of a cloudless blue sky, which he hadn't seen the whole time he had been locked up in an overcrowded prison cell that stank of the sweat and fear of incarcerated men.

The memories of what had happened to him as a teenager had never faded, but Diego had learned to block out thoughts of the past, although he could not prevent his nightmares. He turned his mind to a recent phone call which was the reason for his visit to the convent on the outskirts of Manaus, the largest city in the state of Amazonas.

'I was wondering if you would grant me a favour, Mr Cazorra,' Sister Ann had asked him. And, like a sucker, he'd agreed, thinking that the Mother Superior wanted him to paint some walls or fix the roof. But no, it was nothing so simple. It turned out the favour was to escort one of the nuns to a town on the border with Colombia.

Diego frowned. Torrente was a godforsaken hellhole, and he doubted that a multitude of nuns could make a difference to the lives of the population of the town, who lived in extreme poverty and had pretty much all turned to crime because there was no other way of making money to feed their children.

The *favela* where he had spent his childhood had been as crime-ridden, disease-ridden and despair-ridden as Torrente, and he had no desire to visit a place that was a grim reminder of his past. But he never forgot that the only person who had helped him when he had been a young man in desperate need of salvation had been a priest, Father Vincenzi. Diego was not religious himself, but he felt a strong sense of loyalty to the church that had quite literally taken him from prison and given him his life back.

He was due to return to Rio next week to check up on the casino and nightclub he owned, before flying to Europe for a business meeting with Cruz to discuss his stake in the jewellery company Delgado Diamonds and the Old Betsy diamond mine. But he could spare a couple of days to drive one of the Sisters of the Sacred Heart up to the border. He might even get a chance to take a look at a site where geological survey reports showed there could be gold reserves. Maybe his good turn would be repaid with good luck and he would find gold in Torrente, Diego mused as he adjusted his battered leather hat and climbed out of the Jeep when he saw the door of the convent swing open.

The Mother Superior swept towards him, her grey habit and black veil flapping in the breeze. 'Diego, it's good to see you,' she greeted him in English, which was curious because they normally conversed in their native Portuguese. 'I would like you to meet Sister Clare, who has recently joined our holy order from England.'

So that cleared up one mystery. What was less easy to explain was why his heart felt as if it had slammed into his ribcage with the force of a speeding train. Diego stared at the diminutive figure, dressed from her neck to her ankles in unremitting grey, who followed Sister Ann across the courtyard. Sister Clare's white veil framed a heart-shaped face dominated by the bluest eyes he had ever seen. They had the dark intensity of sapphires, their colour emphasised by the fact that her skin was pale like cream and as flawless as porcelain.

He silently mocked himself. *Santa Mãe*, he'd be writing a sonnet next! He was shocked by his reaction to the English nun and surprised that she was so young. He guessed she was in her early twenties: only a few years older than him when he had been sent to the state penitentiary in Belo Horizonte. Of course prison was not the same as a convent, but he couldn't comprehend why a beautiful young woman would choose to shut herself away from the world.

'I'm pleased to meet you, Mr Cazorra.' Her voice was sweetly melodious, reminding Diego of a crystal-clear mountain stream.

'Sister—' He took off his hat and held out his other hand. He was suddenly conscious of his calloused palm when she placed her fingers in his. Her small hand was swamped by his much bigger one and her skin was as soft as satin. An image flashed into his head of her stroking her soft hands over his naked body. He wondered what her body was like beneath the shapeless nun's habit, which did not entirely conceal the swell of her firm, round breasts.

Whoa! Diego stopped his imagination in its tracks. She was a nun, he reminded himself, and strictly off limits. He was certain he was already damned in the eyes of whatever deity he might meet when the time came for him to leave this world, but having inappropriate thoughts about a holy maid was a step too far even for someone as disreputable as him. But, while he had a conscience, the drug lords in Torrente definitely did not. He doubted they would respect Sister Clare's innocence; they'd just as likely wonder how much money they could make by selling her virginity.

'I can read your thoughts, Diego.' Sister Ann's voice jolted him from those thoughts, and he sincerely hoped she couldn't. 'I can tell you are keen to get on the road before the bad weather that is forecast arrives. When do you estimate you will arrive in Torrente?'

Diego did not want to be responsible for taking the young nun to a town where her safety was by no means guaranteed and he quickly made a decision. 'It's not going to be possible to make the journey, I'm afraid. As you know, the wet season has started early this year and heavy rain is due in the next few days, which will make the roads impassable.'

'But we have to go.' Sister Clare stepped forward and stood directly in front of him. Her petite stature meant that she was forced to tilt her head to look up at him, and Diego was startled by the fierce expression in her blue eyes. 'You agreed to take me.' Her voice was no longer soft and soothing but shrilly demanding. 'I *must* reach Torrente by Sunday.'

He frowned. 'With respect, Sister, you're going there to teach at a Sunday school. It's hardly a matter of life and death and I don't fancy being trapped in Torrente for weeks, possibly months. The road up by the border is a dirt track that turns into a quagmire when it rains.' He jammed his hat on to his head and walked back to his truck. 'I'm sorry. You'll have to start your teaching post next spring when the wet season ends.'

He put his boot on the footplate of the Jeep, but as he was about to swing himself up into the driving seat, he felt a surprisingly firm grip on his arm.

'You're not listening to me, Mr Cazorra. I need to get to Torrente by Sunday and apparently you are the best person to take me. But if you are worried about some wet weather, can you lend me your vehicle so that I can drive myself?'

Diego was riled by Sister Clare's snippy tone. 'Have you seen rain in the Amazon? It's not a light shower like you get in England; it's a deluge that frequently causes flooding and mudslides. I don't allow anyone to drive my truck, Sister. And even if

I did, how would you return it back to me as you'll be living in Torrente?'

Clare bit her lip as she realised her mistake. She could not admit that she intended to catch the first available flight out of Brazil as soon as she had paid the ransom money and rescued Becky. 'I'm sure I could find someone who would drive your Jeep back to Manaus.' Her heart sank as the gold prospector shook his head. She knew of no other way of reaching Becky and this man was her only hope of saving her sister. '*Please*, Mr Cazorra. I *must* get to Torrente.'

Diego cursed beneath his breath when he saw the shimmer of tears in the nun's eyes. He could never resist a pretty face, although his usual response when he was attracted to a woman was to take her to bed until he had sated his desire for her. 'Is teaching at a Sunday school so important to you?'

Sister Clare's sapphire-blue eyes seemed to grow even darker in intensity. 'I…have been called to Torrente,' she said in an emotionally charged voice.

Diego appealed to Sister Ann for support. 'Torrente is a dangerous place, especially for a young woman.'

'Sometimes we are asked to show courage, as the priest who once helped you did,' the Mother Superior reminded him.

'Damn it,' Diego growled. It was true that if Father Vincenzi had not been brave enough to accept the role of chaplain at the violent prison where Diego had been an inmate he might still be rotting in a cell, or dead. Who was he to argue with what the English nun clearly believed was her religious duty?

'*All right.* I'll take you. But don't say I didn't warn you that Torrente is no place for innocents. We'll leave straight away and if we're lucky we might beat the bad weather.'

'Thank you.' Her smile was angelic and Diego felt a strange sensation in his chest as if a hand was squeezing his heart. His gaze dropped once more to the outline of her pert breasts and he felt as though another part of his anatomy was being squeezed! He'd obviously gone too long without sex, he thought derisively. When he went back to Rio he would remedy the situation and visit one of his casual mistresses, many of whom were dancers who worked at his nightclub.

His life as a wealthy entrepreneur was very different from the poverty and deprivation he had endured as a child, Diego mused. His mother had been a drug addict, and most of the time she'd been incapable of taking care of her son. From a young age, Diego had been left to roam the dark alleyways of the *favela*. He had witnessed things that no child should see, and sometimes when he'd felt really scared he'd taken shelter at his friend Cruz Delgado's home. By the time he was a teenager he had become hardened to the grim realities of life in a slum, but one night he had found his mother being beaten by her drug dealer because she did not have enough money to pay him, and Diego had lost his temper—with catastrophic results.

Deus, don't go there! He jerked his mind away from the dark pit of his past and glanced towards the Mother Superior, who had gone back inside the convent and now returned carrying a crate filled with bottles of drinking water. 'You'll need to take plenty of fluids with you for the trip,' she said.

Diego preferred a stronger kind of liquid refreshment, but he shrugged. 'Pack the water in the back of the Jeep,' he told Sister Clare, 'while I check over the engine.'

Clare's hands were shaking as she gripped the crate of water bottles, and her legs felt so wobbly that when she climbed into the back of the Jeep she sank on to her knees, overcome with relief that she had persuaded the prospector to drive her to Torrente. She was a vital step closer to rescuing Becky. Her heart was beating painfully hard in her chest, but not only from fear of what lay ahead when she met the kidnappers.

When the Mother Superior had said the gold prospector was a womaniser, Clare had visualised the slimeball taxi driver who had flirted with her when he had driven her to the convent. She could not have been more wrong! Diego Cazorra was the most gorgeous man she had ever seen. Working for her parents' modelling agency meant that she had met hundreds of good-looking guys, but none, including Mark, came close to the smoulderingly sexy Brazilian.

She studied him through the window of the Jeep. The first thing that had struck her about him was his height. He was several inches over six feet tall, lean-hipped, his long legs encased in faded denim jeans, which he wore with calf-length leather boots. His broad shoulders and powerful pectoral muscles were clearly defined beneath his tight-fitting black T-shirt.

The biggest surprise was when he had removed his hat and revealed an unruly mass of streaked dark blond hair that reached to below his collar. His European appearance was further enhanced by his silvery-grey eyes and sculpted features: razor-edged cheekbones and a square jaw covered by several days' growth of blond stubble. Add to that a blatantly sensual mouth and a wicked glint in his eyes when his gaze had lingered on her breasts that had made Clare feel flustered.

He was a fallen angel and he oozed sex appeal from every pore, but she was horrified by her reaction to the prospector when her thoughts should be totally focused on Becky. Even if Sister Ann hadn't warned her that he was a womaniser, she would have guessed as much from the way he had eyed her up as if he was imagining her without any clothes on. She could still feel a tingling sensation in her breasts and was thankful that the stiff serge fabric of her nun's habit disguised the hard points of her nipples. Suddenly the Mother Superior's advice to travel to Torrente in the guise of a nun seemed a good idea. She could not afford any distractions.

The slam of the Jeep's bonnet made Clare jump and she looked around for somewhere to store the bottles of water. There were no seats in the back of the Jeep, just a bench running down one side, a camping stove and cooking equipment and a couple of rolled-up sleeping bags. The Jeep was basic, but as long as it got her to Torrente she didn't care that it promised to be an uncomfortable ride.

The storage area behind the front seats already contained a large crate of beers. She moved the crate over to make room for the water bottles and discovered a pile of books and, out of curiosity, she glanced at the titles and was surprised to see her favourite novel, *Great Expectations* by Charles Dickens. There were a number of other classic novels by Orwell, Steinbeck and Tolstoy. She would not have guessed that the tough gold prospector's choice of reading material included *Anna Karenina*, the iconic tale of doomed love—which just went to prove the adage that you shouldn't judge a book by its cover, she mused, as she flipped through a well-thumbed book of poetry by John Keats before replacing it where she had found it.

The prospector called her, sounding impatient. 'Are you holding a prayer meeting back there? Let's go, Sister.'

Clare hurried round to the front of the Jeep and

her heart gave a painful lurch when she realised that the briefcase containing the ransom money was no longer where she had left it on the floor of the court-yard.

'Where is my case?' she demanded in a panic-stricken voice.

'I put it on the front seat.' The prospector gave her a curious look. 'Take it easy. What are you carrying in that case that is so valuable—the Crown Jewels?' he asked in a teasing voice.

Five hundred thousand pounds to save her sister's life. Clare swallowed. 'Books for the Sunday school.' Technically, it wasn't a lie. Sister Ann *had* given her a few prayer books to take to Father Roberto, the priest in Torrente.

She was relieved to see the briefcase in the front of the Jeep. There was no elegant way of climbing up into the cab. She hitched her nun's habit up to her knees so that she could put her foot on to the step, and gave a startled gasp when two hands gripped her waist and the prospector lifted her off the ground.

For a few breathless seconds she was aware of the strength of his arms around her and the imprint of his fingers burned through the stiff fabric of her clothes and set her skin on fire. The scent of san-dalwood cologne mixed with his musky maleness stirred her senses, and she felt an inexplicable urge to turn her head and press her lips against the blond stubble on his jaw.

'Thank you, Mr Cazorra,' she mumbled as he

plonked her on to the passenger seat. Her face felt hot with embarrassment that he might have guessed her thoughts.

'Any time,' he said laconically. 'My name's Diego. We're going to be spending the next forty-eight hours together so let's drop the formality.'

'Forty-eight hours! Do you mean we won't reach Torrente today?' Clare stared at him and her stomach swooped as her eyes were drawn to the lazy curl of his smile. 'Where will we spend tonight?'

'I usually sleep in the back of the Jeep. Admittedly, it's not very comfortable for someone of my height, but it does for a night or two.'

Clare pictured herself and the prospector squashed into the small space and her heart gave a painful jolt. 'I can't sleep in the Jeep with you.'

Diego silently acknowledged the truth of her statement. There was only one reason he would spend a night with a woman and it certainly wasn't to sleep. Various inappropriate thoughts had run through his mind when he had lifted Sister Clare into the Jeep. His hands had almost spanned her tiny waist and he had been aware of the gentle flare of her hips and the swell of her breasts. He guessed that beneath the voluminous folds of her nun's habit she had the curvaceous figure of a Pocket Venus, but he would have to curb his imagination or spend the five-hundred-mile journey to Torrente in his current uncomfortable state of arousal.

'There is a settlement on the way to Torrente where we'll stop tonight. The villagers offer basic accommodation for tourists who want to explore the rainforest.'

He started the engine and Sister Ann spoke to Clare. 'Good luck, my dear. I will pray for your safe-keeping and for your soul.'

As the Jeep turned out of the convent grounds Clare was gripped with apprehension that soon she would meet the kidnappers. She felt sad to be leaving the Sisters of the Sacred Heart, knowing she was unlikely to meet them again.

'Good luck?' Diego questioned. 'Torrente must be an even worse place than it was the last time I visited the town if the Mother Superior needs to pray for you while you teach at the Sunday school.'

He glanced at his passenger and wondered why she blushed. The soft stain of colour on her face emphasised the delicate lines of her cheekbones and made her look even lovelier. But something about the situation didn't feel right. He had an antenna for trouble, honed during his years living in the *favela* and the time he had spent in prison. His experiences of life had turned him into a cynic, he acknowledged. What could be suspect about a young nun who was as pure and beautiful as an English rose?

'It was a figure of speech.' Sister Clare turned her guileless blue eyes to him. 'I'm sure Sister Ann prays for all souls, even yours, Mr Cazorra.'

He dismissed his strange feeling that she was not what she seemed and grinned. 'Heck, that's going to take a lot of prayers.'

CHAPTER TWO

CLARE WAS DETERMINED not to respond to the gold prospector's undeniable charisma. She looked away from his toe-tingling smile to focus on the road ahead. The highway was signposted to Boa Vista, which she remembered from the map was in the far north of Brazil, but soon they turned off the main road on to a dirt track.

'There are no paved roads going west,' Diego explained. 'Most people who want to visit the towns along the border with Colombia and Peru travel by boat on the Rio Negro.'

'Why didn't we take a boat instead of driving?'

'The river narrows as it flows into Torrente, making it easy for the drug lords to control the area. There's an airstrip at the edge of the town which they also control. Travelling by Jeep means I can go where I like and, more importantly, I can leave whenever I want to.'

Clare's heart plummeted at the news that criminals controlled the air and river routes into and out of Torrente. Once she had paid the ransom money she hoped to get Becky to safety as quickly as possible. She wondered if she should tell the prospector the real reason she was going to the town and maybe he would agree to bring her and Becky back to Manaus. But, although Sister Ann had said he was trustworthy, Clare was afraid to trust anyone apart from the nuns who had helped her.

She thought of her father back in London. Rory Marchant would be desperately waiting for news of Becky but trying to pretend to his wife that there was nothing wrong. Tammi Marchant was only in her early fifties, but a year ago she had suffered a stroke that had left her partially paralysed. It broke Clare's heart to see her once vibrant and still beautiful mother now so fragile. Her father had insisted on caring full-time for his wife and had handed the running of A-Star PR over to Clare.

It had been a daunting task to take charge of the agency, but Clare had risen to the challenge. She'd enjoyed developing her PR skills and had discovered a natural talent for devising advertising campaigns. At least being busy meant she'd had no time to brood over her break-up with Mark. Her mother's illness and her father's devoted care of his wife had shown her that she wanted a marriage as strong as her parents' relationship, and she was prepared to hold out until she met a man she could love and trust with all her heart.

The one positive thing was that recently she had felt a deepening bond with her father as they'd shared looking after Tammi and discussed business together. For the first time in her life she sensed that her father was as proud of her as he was of her sister. Of course she was not in the same league as Becky, who was one of the world's most sought-after models, but it made a nice change to realise that being the brainy daughter rather than the beautiful one wasn't such a bad thing.

It was likely that Becky's fame and high profile were the reasons she had been targeted by the kidnappers. Perhaps they had tied Becky up—or worse, Clare thought sickly, as she remembered the severed piece of earlobe the kidnappers had sent her.

She took a deep breath and tried to calm herself down. Allowing her imagination to run away with her would not help Becky. In an attempt to take her mind off the situation she searched for a topic of conversation.

'What exactly does a gold prospector do? I mean, I realise that you search for gold, but there must be more to it than that.'

'Actually, it's pretty much as you described. I take my metal detector to areas where I think there might be gold deposits.'

'But how do you know where to start looking?'

'I have a good knowledge of geology and I know how to recognise signs of mineralisation. I carry equipment that allows me to analyse rocks, but often it's down to intuition. I've been looking for, and mining, gold and diamonds for many years.'

Clare's eyes were drawn to the prospector's darkly tanned fingers on the steering wheel and she recalled that when she had shaken his hand the skin on his palm had felt rough, as if he was used to manual work. 'Have you actually worked in mines? What made you choose such a dangerous job?'

He shrugged. 'I needed to make a living, but I left school with few qualifications, which limited my career options,' he said drily. 'Mining is dangerous but it's well paid.'

A poorly educated miner who read Tolstoy and poetry? Clare studied his chiselled profile and wondered where he had learned to speak faultless English, albeit with a sexy accent. She flushed when he turned his head and caught her looking at him. 'You obviously lead an interesting life, Mr Cazorra,' she murmured.

'My name is Diego,' he reminded her. 'I've got a question for you, Sister. What made you decide to become a nun?'

Oh, help. She bit her lip as she searched her mind for an answer.

'If you don't mind me saying so, you are a beautiful young woman and committing yourself to a life of chastity is not normal, in my opinion.'

She shot him a startled glance at the same time as he turned his head towards her, and their eyes met. Once again she was aware of a sizzle of sexual chemistry between them. Did he really think she was beautiful? For years she had compared her very

ordinary features to her sister's stunning looks and
she had never had much self-confidence in her appearance.

The Mother Superior had warned her that the
prospector was a womaniser, Clare reminded herself. He probably flirted with every woman he met,
but even if he did find her attractive, she could not
respond to the gleam in his eyes without blowing her
cover that she was a nun. She realised he was waiting for her to answer his question, but lying did not
come naturally to her.

'All of us are on a personal journey, and this is the
road I have chosen to take,' she said vaguely. It was
not entirely untruthful because the road to Torrente
led to her sister. She was eager to change the subject and at that moment a flock of brightly coloured
birds flew out of the trees.

'Oh, look! Are they parrots? I've only ever seen
a parrot in a cage. There is such a huge diversity of
wildlife in the rainforest. I recently watched a docu-
mentary about the Amazon. Did you know that over
a thousand species of birds are found in the Amazon
basin?' Clare was determined to keep the prospector's
attention away from her personal life. 'Sister Ann said
you know the rainforest well. I suppose you must get
the chance to see many different species of wildlife?'

He gave another shrug. 'I've hunted wild boar occasionally if I needed a meal and run out of supplies.
And it's always a good idea to check your sleeping

bag before you get into it in case a tarantula has crawled inside.'

'Really?' Clare paled. 'I hate spiders.' She winced as the Jeep hit a pothole in the road and she was jolted in her seat, only saved from hitting her head on the window by her seat belt. The dirt road was becoming progressively bumpier as they drove further west, and the trees on either side grew so densely that in places they formed a tunnel that the sunlight could barely penetrate. She did not want to think about spiders or any other deadly creatures that might be lurking in the humid gloom of the forest. Nor did she want to think of the evil men who had snatched Becky. She forced her mind to more pleasant thoughts. 'I believe there are many different species of monkeys living in the rainforest. Do you like monkeys, Mr Cazorra?'

'To eat?' he drawled.

'Of course not. You don't really eat monkeys, do you?' She gave him a horrified look, only realising when he grinned that he was teasing her. His smile should come with a danger warning, she thought, feeling the hard points of her nipples chafe against her lacy bra. Her inconvenient awareness of the prospector was making a stressful situation even worse. She could not bring herself to use his first name, preferring to keep a sense of formality between them. With a deep sigh, she turned her head and stared out of the window to remark on interesting flora and fauna as the Jeep bounced along the uneven road.

They had been travelling for a couple of hours when the first drops of rain landed on the windscreen and quickly turned the dust-covered glass opaque, despite the efforts of the windscreen wipers.

Diego cursed beneath his breath as within seconds the shower became a torrential downpour. From experience he knew the potholes in the road would soon fill up and the road would turn into a river of mud. He needed all his concentration to drive in these conditions, but his passenger hadn't stopped talking for what seemed like eternity.

'Sister Clare—' he interrupted her mid flow as she listed some of the different types of flowers that apparently grew in the rainforest; the woman was a walking encyclopedia '—have you ever considered joining a silent order?'

She blushed and Diego was fascinated by the rosy stain that spread across her cheeks. He couldn't remember ever seeing a woman blush before, but the kind of women he associated with were not sweet virgins, he acknowledged. He pictured Sister Clare's pretty face flushed with a glow of sexual arousal and shifted uncomfortably in his seat as his body reacted predictably.

'I'm sorry.' She nibbled her lower lip with her teeth, making Diego long to soothe the tender flesh with his tongue. 'I tend to talk too much when I'm nervous,' she admitted.

'You're right to be nervous. Torrente is not a nice place.' He wished she had taken heed of what he'd told her about the town before they had left Manaus. 'If you want to turn back, say so now. Once the road floods, I won't be able to turn the Jeep round without the risk of the tyres becoming stuck in the mud.'

'We can't turn back!' Panic made Clare's voice sharp. The prospector gave her a curious glance and she forced herself to speak in a calmer tone. 'I want to carry on to Torrente. I have a job to do there.'

'Couldn't you have taught at a Sunday school in England?' he muttered, followed by something in Portuguese, and Clare guessed it was a good thing she did not understand.

He had been right about the rain in the Amazon being a deluge. Five minutes ago the sun had been shining, but now it was as if a dam had burst and gallons of water were falling on to the Jeep and the road, which, as she peered through the windscreen, she could see was quickly becoming a river of mud.

She was jolted violently as the wheels went down another pothole and the truck came to a standstill. Diego revved the engine but the Jeep did not move and, looking out of the side window, Clare saw the wheels spinning round in the mud. When he rammed the gear lever into reverse she held her breath as the Jeep moved backwards a little way before it stopped.

'What are we going to do?' Clare had to shout above the noise of the rain hitting the roof. 'I thought the bad weather wasn't due for a few days?'

'It rains every day in the rainforest,' Diego said ironically. 'This shower will probably last for an

hour. When the wet season starts properly it sometimes rains for days without stopping.'

'I suppose we'll have to wait until the rain stops
before we can try to dig the wheels out of the mud?'

'If we wait, the Jeep will sink up to the axles in
no time. I've got some wooden planks in the back
that I'll put under the rear tyres.'

Diego pulled the brim of his hat down low to
shield his eyes from the rain and opened the door.
Within seconds of stepping out of the Jeep he was
soaked to the skin. 'Slide across to the driver's seat,'
he ordered Clare. 'When you hear me thump twice
on the Jeep I want you to start the engine, select reverse gear and then accelerate slowly.' He looked at
her closely. 'Do you know how to drive a car?'

'Yes, of course I do.' She had never driven a four-
by-four or attempted to free a vehicle that was stuck
in mud, but Clare tried to sound more confident than
she felt. After some fumbling, she found reverse gear
and when she heard two thumps on the bodywork
she pressed her foot down on the accelerator pedal.
Nothing happened, so she pressed harder until finally the Jeep rolled backwards.

They were free! Feeling a sense of achievement,
she smiled at the prospector when he yanked open
the door, but her smile faded as she took in his mud-
spattered appearance.

'Santa Mãe! I told you to accelerate slowly. Look
at me.'

Clare couldn't stop looking at him! Even covered

CHANTELLE SHAW 37

in mud he was the sexiest man she had ever laid eyes
on. She shifted across to the passenger seat so that
he could climb into the Jeep. There was even mud
on his face, but he still looked gorgeous and he exuded an air of toughness and raw masculinity that
made Clare imagine being swept up into his arms
and carried off to be thoroughly ravished by him.

His T-shirt was sodden and her heart skipped a
beat when he pulled it off to reveal his tanned chest,
covered with a fuzz of golden hairs. Heaven help
her. He had an amazing body. She could not tear
her eyes from his well-defined six-pack and powerful shoulder muscles. Her parents would snap him
up on to A-Star PR's books, but she would feel a lot
more comfortable if his toned physique was hidden
from her view. 'Do you have a spare shirt I could find
for you?' Her voice sounded annoyingly breathless.

'There's no point. It's likely the Jeep will get stuck
again and I'll have to get out in the rain to free up
the wheels.' His eyes narrowed on her pink cheeks.
'Next time, could you not stamp on the accelerator
like you're a racing car driver?'

She was already overwrought with worry about
Becky and felt ultra-sensitive to his criticism. 'I'm
sorry you got covered in mud, but I thought you
wanted to get the Jeep out of the pothole,' she said
stiffly.

'You have no idea what I want, Sister,' Diego muttered. If she did not stop looking at him like she was
doing—as if she had never seen a half-naked male

before—he would be unable to restrain himself from showing her *exactly* what he wanted.

He dragged his gaze from her cupid's-bow lips and tried not to imagine how soft and moist her mouth would feel beneath his if he kissed her. It was likely she had never seen a man's bare flesh, he conceded. His skin was burning up, but for the first time in his life he could not succumb to temptation. If she had been any other woman he would have suggested they climb into the back of the Jeep so that they could alleviate their mutual desire.

For it *was* mutual. Diego's extensive experience of women meant he was infallible at recognising the telltale signs of sexual awareness. Sister Clare was desperately trying to hide her reaction to the chemistry fizzing between them, but her big blue eyes reflected her sexual interest in him that her chosen way of life commanded her to deny.

Deus, women were always trouble, he thought, reaching behind the seat for a beer. He flipped off the bottle top with the opener that, for convenience, he had screwed to the Jeep's dashboard and lifted the bottle towards his lips but, before he could take a swig, a hand grabbed his arm.

'Surely you are not thinking of drinking alcohol while you're driving?' Clare said in an outraged voice.

'I'd prefer not to be thinking about it, Sister,' Diego murmured as he lifted the bottle closer to his mouth and felt her fingers dig into his bicep. Her hand looked pale against his darkly tanned skin. He visualised her naked white body beneath him, her soft thighs spread in readiness for him to possess her. Tension coiled low in his gut and he shrugged her hand from his arm and put the bottle to his lips, his taste buds anticipating his first sip of beer. It was warm rather than ice-cold the way he liked it, but it was better than nothing.

Diego stiffened when Clare leaned across him and he inhaled a fresh lemony fragrance, which he recognised was soap. He supposed nuns did not wear perfume or make-up. Sister Clare's smooth complexion was entirely natural. Her long eyelashes were dark auburn and he wondered if her hair, hidden beneath her veil, was the same colour.

The jangling sound of metal jerked Diego from his fantasies and he frowned when he saw that she had taken the keys out of the ignition.

'Drunk driving is a despicable crime and potentially life-threatening to other road users,' she stated.

He tried to control his impatience. 'In normal circumstances I agree that driving after drinking alcohol is unacceptable, certainly in a town. But, in case you hadn't noticed, we are the only people on the road. We haven't seen another vehicle since we left Manaus, and we won't see another one because no one else is crazy enough to want to go to Torrente.'

He held out his hand. 'Give me the keys, Sister Clare, and let's be on our way. We can't afford any more delays if you want to reach Torrente by Sunday.'

She *had* to be there on Sunday to pay Becky's ransom. Clare remembered the instructions from the kidnappers to wait in a cave close to a waterfall just outside the town. She felt torn, knowing the gold prospector was right and they could not afford to be delayed. But she fervently believed that driving while under the influence of alcohol was wrong.

'My aunt was killed by a drunk driver,' she burst out. 'Aunt Edith was knocked off her bicycle one Christmas Eve. The driver of the car who was responsible for her death was found to be three times over the legal alcohol limit.'

Diego squinted through the mud-smeared windscreen at the torrential rain. 'I'm sorry about your aunt, but we're unlikely to come across a cyclist in the middle of the rainforest.' He looked at Clare, noting the stubborn set of her chin but also the faint quiver of her lower lip. She had the most beautiful eyes, twin sapphires that at this moment shimmered with a sheen of tears. 'Damn it.' He exhaled heavily. *'All right,'* he muttered as he wound down the window and poured the beer on to the ground.

'Satisfied?' He glared at Clare as she silently handed him the keys.

The word hovered in the hot, humid atmosphere inside the Jeep as sexual tension exploded between them. Clare's gaze locked with the prospector's grey eyes. *Satisfied* made her think wanton thoughts and imagine how it would feel to be satisfied by him. With his rugged good looks and to-die-for body, he was every woman's fantasy and, without consciously being aware of moving, she swayed towards him, her eyes unknowingly issuing an invitation as she moistened her dry lips with the tip of her tongue.

Seemingly in slow motion, he lowered his head until his face was so near to hers that she felt the whisper of his breath on her cheek. Another few centimetres and his mouth would brush across her lips. She held her breath, willing him, wanting him to kiss her.

Suddenly Becky's face flashed into her mind. Dear heaven, *what was she doing?* Clare silently questioned. Self-disgust swept through her as she realised she had not given her sister a thought while she had been panting over the gold prospector.

She jerked away from him and inched across her seat until she could go no further and was pressed up against the door. 'Please, can we continue our journey, Mr Cazorra?' she said in a low voice.

For a moment she thought he was going to refuse. When she peeped at him she was shocked by the feral hunger that tautened his features and gave him a wolf-like appearance that was further enhanced by the hungry gleam in his eyes. She was relieved when he inserted the key into the ignition and started the engine.

Diego forced himself to concentrate on steering the Jeep around the rain-filled potholes. It was impossible to tell how deep the holes were and he wanted to avoid becoming stuck in the mud again at all costs.

The quicker they got to Torrente and he could deliver his beautiful, infuriating passenger, the better it would suit him.

He glanced at her sitting primly beside him, her body hidden by her nun's habit and her hair covered by her veil so that only her lovely face was visible. Her serene expression irked him. She was apparently unaffected by the fact that they had been a heartbeat away from kissing, while he was aware of a dull ache in his groin that felt as if he'd been kicked by a mule.

'You seem to have trouble remembering my name, Sister Clare,' he drawled. 'I'll remind you again. It's Diego. If you call me Mr Cazorra once more, I might be tempted to assist your memory.'

'Assist, how?' Clare was curious, despite her determination to keep her distance from him, something that was difficult to do physically while they were cooped up in the Jeep. She was intensely aware of him every time he moved his arm to change gear, and when he took off his hat and ran his hand through his hair, her fingers itched to brush back the dark blond strands that had fallen across his brow.

He took his eyes briefly from the road and sent her a smouldering glance that melted her insides. 'I'll have to kiss you until you have learned my name.'

CHAPTER THREE

HEAT SWEPT THROUGH Clare and she felt herself blush from the tips of her ears down to her toes as she visualised Diego carrying out his threat. This had to stop, she told herself firmly. She had come to Brazil for one reason only—to rescue Becky. She had no idea what kind of conditions her sister was being held in, but the severed piece of earlobe sent to her by the kidnappers made the situation very real and very dangerous. She could not allow herself to be distracted by the outrageously sexy man sitting beside her.

Unable to think of a suitable retort to what she assumed was his teasing remark, she turned her head to stare out of the window at the unending jungle. He would not really dare kiss her, she assured herself. But she remembered the Mother Superior's warning about him being a womaniser and decided not to give him any opportunity to take liberties with her.

They had been driving for some while—Clare had been absorbed in her thoughts and had lost all

track of time—when the rain stopped as suddenly as
it had started. The heat of the sun close to the equa-
tor caused the wet leaves to evaporate steam into
the air so that the forest looked like a giant smoking
cauldron. Even the huge puddles were steaming on
the road that stretched ahead as far as the eye could
see, like a giant brown snake wending through the
green forest.

'When was your aunt killed?' Diego asked suddenly, his voice breaking the tense silence that had
filled the Jeep for miles.

'Almost two years ago.' Clare remembered the
cold grey day before Christmas when her mother had
phoned to break the news that Aunt Edith had died
after being knocked off her bike by a car. The fact
that the driver was drunk at the time of the accident
had only been revealed later at the inquest, and Clare
had felt anger as well as grief that her aunt's life had
been ended by a thoughtless, selfish act.

It was hard to imagine that when she had left England three days ago the weather had, typically for
November, been freezing cold with the promise of
sleet, while in Brazil the temperature on the dashboard was showing thirty-seven degrees centigrade
and the humidity was so high that Clare's clothes
were sticking to her.

'The car driver said that he skidded on a patch
of ice, but the police breathalysed him and found he
was over the alcohol limit and shouldn't have been
driving,' she said tautly. 'My aunt was older than

my parents, but she was fit and healthy until her life was cut short.'

'You were obviously fond of her.'

It was strange how it was often the way that you didn't appreciate what you had until it was gone, Clare mused. She missed Aunt Edith's sensible advice and dry humour more than she would have believed.

'I lived with her for part of my childhood.' She gave a rueful smile. 'At the time I hated being packed off to her cottage in a remote Kent village while my parents remained at our home in London. It never occurred to me that my aunt might not have enjoyed having her life disrupted by a stroppy kid.'

'Why did your parents send you away from home?' Diego could not explain why he was curious about his passenger. Usually he avoided personal discussions. He was never even mildly interested in his mistresses' private lives, and he discouraged curiosity about himself. His past was not a place he wanted to revisit or reveal to anyone.

'My sister was very ill when she was a child. She was diagnosed with leukaemia when she was six years old and underwent chemotherapy for several years before she was finally given the all-clear. My parents couldn't cope with spending weeks, sometimes months, in the hospital with Becky at the same time as trying to run their PR company and look after me.'

She sighed. 'It sounds ridiculous, but I felt aban-

doned by my parents. I was only nine when Becky
became ill, and I didn't understand how serious her
illness was. When my parents spent so much time
with her I believed she was their favourite child.'

'That's understandable.' Diego could appreciate
Clare's feeling of abandonment when she was a child.
He had been abandoned by his father before he had
been born, and his mother's dependence on crack
cocaine meant that he had learned to fend for himself from a young age. 'You said your sister made a
full recovery. Once she was better, did you return
to live with your parents?'

'No. I visited them at weekends, but I had started
at a secondary school in Kent and my parents decided it would be better not to disrupt my education
by moving me to a new school in London.'

'You must have resented your sister because she
lived with your parents while you were left with your
aunt.'

Clare was surprised by Diego's perception. There
had been times when she had felt jealous of all the
attention Becky received, she acknowledged, but she
had hated herself for her jealousy because, of course,
her sister had not chosen to have leukaemia.

'I love my sister. It wasn't Becky's fault that I
grew up feeling pushed out of the family. I was lucky
that I hadn't been struck down with a horrible illness or spent chunks of my childhood in the hospital. My parents dealt with a difficult situation in the
best way they could.'

Thinking about Becky and wondering if the kidnappers had harmed her made Clare's stomach contract. Becky had suffered so much as a child and it
seemed desperately unfair that once again her life
was threatened. Clare hoped her sister was not making the situation even more difficult. Becky had been
over-indulged by their parents during the long years
of her illness, and her subsequent career as a successful model meant that she was used to people rushing
around after her. But it was unlikely the kidnappers
would treat Becky like a princess.

The Jeep lurched as the wheels went down another
crater in the road and Clare winced and rubbed her
bruised spine. The continual jolting made her feel
as though she was inside the drum of a washing ma-
chine on the fast spin cycle.

'How much longer do you think it will take us
to reach the village where we are going to stop for
the night?'

Diego glanced at the instrument panel. 'We've
driven one hundred and forty miles. Inua village is
two hundred and fifty miles from Manaus and because of the damned potholes in the road we're travelling at an average speed of thirty-five miles an hour.'

'So we should reach the village in just over three
hours,' Clare said instantly. She caught Diego's surprised look. 'I have a freakish brain when it comes
to maths. At school, when my friends were trying to
decide what careers to choose, I always knew that I
wanted to be an accountant.'

'So, did you go to university?'

She nodded. 'I have a degree in Accountancy and Marketing and after I graduated I was headhunted by a top bank in the City of London. I worked for the bank for eighteen months, before I became chief accountant at my parents' public relations company. Recently, I've become much more involved in the actual PR side of the business.'

Diego frowned. 'I'm trying to understand what made you give up a good career and cut yourself off from your family and friends. How do your parents feel about your decision, especially as you have chosen to leave England and join a holy order in Brazil?'

Clare regretted telling him so much about herself. It was a sign of her insecurity that she felt she needed to boast of her academic achievements to make up for the fact that she wasn't beautiful, she acknowledged ruefully. For a few moments she had forgotten that the Mother Superior had persuaded her to pretend to be a nun for her protection. She felt uncomfortable about her deception but she did not dare risk telling Diego the real reason why she was going to Torrente.

'My parents support what I am doing,' she murmured, remembering how her father had hugged her tightly when she'd said goodbye to him before leaving for Brazil. 'What about you?' She steered the conversation away from herself. 'Do you have a family?'

'No.'

When it became clear that Diego wasn't going to add anything more, Clare tried again. 'So, you're not married?'

'No.'

'I imagine being a gold prospector means you spend a lot of time on your own. It must be a lonely way of life.'

'I like my own company,' he drawled.

Clare gave up. She wanted to ask him how he had developed an appreciation of classic literature if his education had been as poor as he had said. There was something about him that made her think he was more than a rough, tough prospector. It was not just because of the books she had found. She could not explain why she sensed an air of mystery about him, but the idea that he was hiding something reinforced her decision to keep the truth about her identity a secret.

The surface of the dirt road grew worse the further west they travelled. Twice more the Jeep became embedded in mud. The first time, Diego managed to free the wheels by placing wooden planks beneath them, but on the second occasion he had to use a specially designed jack to lift up the front of the Jeep. It was a lengthy procedure and Clare had to get out to help and found herself ankle-deep in mud which dried to the consistency of cement in the sun.

By the time they reached Inua she was wilting

from the humidity and exhaustion and visualised a clean hotel room, hopefully with air conditioning and perhaps even a bath.

'Where is the rest of the village?' she asked Diego when he parked in a clearing in the forest where a few huts with thatched roofs were grouped around a larger hut that seemed to be a communal place for the villagers. The men sitting on the floor outside the large hut were mainly dressed in shorts and shirts, but the women were topless and the children who rushed up to greet the white-skinned strangers simply wore loincloths.

'This is it,' Diego told her. 'Inua is home to a small community called the Yanomami.'

'But you said that tourists stay here.' Clare looked at the ramshackle huts. 'Where will I sleep tonight?' Her visions of a comfortable bedroom and en suite bathroom were disappearing.

'The guest hut is over there.' Diego pointed to a hut set slightly apart from the others. 'Don't worry,' he said when he saw her expression. 'The wooden cubicle next to the hut is a shower. The Yanomami children find the shower fascinating because they bathe in the river.'

He walked away to talk to an elderly tribesman and came back to Clare a few minutes later. 'I'll get your bag from the Jeep and show you your accommodation. The tribal elder, Jacinto, asked if we would like to eat dinner with the Yanomami people, but they do actually hunt monkey and that's what's

on tonight's menu. I guessed you'd want me to de-
cline the invitation.'

'Thank you.' Clare shuddered. She hadn't felt like
eating much since she had heard about Becky being
kidnapped, and the idea of eating monkey destroyed
all vestiges of her appetite. She followed Diego into
the guest hut and was relieved to see a wooden bed
frame. The mattress was woefully thin, but at least
she would not have to sleep on the floor.

'I realise it's not the New York Hilton,' Diego
drawled when he saw her expression, 'but I assume
you are used to living a simple life at the convent.'

She looked at him suspiciously. 'How does a gold
prospector and self-confessed loner know what the
New York Hilton is like?'

He gave her one of his heart-stopping grins and
ignored her question. 'I'm going to cook dinner
on the camping stove. I only have non-perishable
tinned food, nothing fancy. But you're welcome to
join me.'

'Actually, I think I'll have a shower and an early
night. It's been a tiring day.' The heat and her constant worry about Becky had made her feel drained
both physically and emotionally. Her fierce awareness of Diego was not helping matters, Clare conceded as she watched him walk over to the Jeep. A
brief spectacular sunset had streaked the sky with
hues of pink and orange, but now darkness was
closing in and she felt very alone in an alien envi-
ronment.

It was a relief to take off the stiff serge habit and her veil. The shower was surprisingly powerful, but Clare was convinced she had glimpsed a snake slither out of the cubicle as she had entered and she did not dare hang around in case it came back.

Even at night the humidity was so high that she felt as if she was being smothered in a damp blanket. She had packed a light cotton chemise to sleep in, but she was still too hot and the mosquitoes were eating her alive. She lay on the bed, huddled beneath the mosquito net, and wondered where Becky was sleeping tonight. The rainforest was even noisier at night than during the day, as hundreds of species of insects and nocturnal creatures vied to make the loudest sounds.

What was that? Clare tensed when she heard a scurrying noise on the floor of the hut. Could it be a rat? Her muscles tensed and her heart was pounding. The noise came again and she switched on her torch and shone it on the floor. The beam of light revealed a huge cockroach, its hard black shell gleaming and its long antennae twitching as it moved purposefully towards the bed.

'Ugh!' Clare's nerve crumbled. The rainforest was a terrifying place. She loved the English countryside, but here in the jungle she imagined what other creatures might be crawling or slithering inside the hut. Panic engulfed her and, without thinking of anything but her desperate need to find a place of safety, she leapt out of bed and remembered to grab the brief-

case containing the ransom money before she tore out of the hut. She sprinted over to the Jeep faster than she had ever run in her life. The rough ground hurt her bare feet and the beam from her torch picked out glowing pinpricks of light that she realised were the eyes of animals hiding in the dark forest. Frantic with fear, she pulled open the back door of the Jeep.

'*Diego*, there's a *huge* cockroach in the hut.' She paused to drag oxygen into her lungs—and stared.

Diego was sprawled on top of a mattress that he had unrolled to cover the floor of the Jeep. He was leaning back against a couple of cushions, bare chested, his jeans sitting low on his hips. A kerosene lamp emitted a bright glow that fell on the pages of the book he was reading and cast a pool of light on his torso, highlighting the golden hairs on his chest. With his tousled blond hair and the blond stubble on his jaw, he reminded Clare of a lion: sleek, muscular and supremely powerful.

'Unlikely,' he drawled in his laid-back manner that gave the impression he took nothing in life too seriously.

'There *is*. I know what a cockroach looks like.'

'I meant it's unlikely there's only one. Cockroaches like company and they like to hide in small spaces. There is probably a nest of them behind the headboard of the bed.'

Clare shuddered. 'I can't sleep in the hut with a family of cockroaches.' She screamed as she felt something touch her foot. *'There's a snake on me. It's running up my leg!'*

'Snakes don't run.' Diego held up the lamp so that it shone on the ground where Clare was standing. 'It's just a harmless lizard,' he told her as he brushed the vivid green creature from her leg. 'It's probably far more scared of you than you are of it.'

'I wouldn't bank on it,' Clare muttered as she scrambled into the Jeep, unaware that as she did so the hem of her chemise slid up to reveal several inches of her bare thighs. She pushed her mane of long auburn hair out of her eyes and looked pleadingly at Diego. 'Please can I sleep in here tonight?'

He did not reply and she wondered why he was staring at her as if she had grown another head. 'What's wrong?' she said shakily. 'Do I have another lizard on me?'

'I thought nuns had to cut their hair short.'

Idiot, Clare silently berated herself. She had forgotten that she wasn't wearing her nun's habit and veil. Her hair had dried quickly after her shower, but the humidity and the fact that she did not have her straighteners had resulted in a wild tangle of curls tumbling halfway down her back. She tensed as Diego reached out and wound a curl around his fingers.

'It feels like silk,' he murmured. 'And it's such an amazing colour. It reminds me of the conkers I saw children collecting in England when I was there one autumn.' His eyes narrowed on Clare's flushed face. 'It's a pity to hide such beautiful hair beneath a veil.'

She sensed he was waiting for an explanation and searched her mind for one. 'I'm a novice, which is why I wear a white veil instead of a black one. I don't have to cut my hair until I take my final vows.'

'When will you do that?'

'Soon,' she assured him quickly.

Diego shut the door of the Jeep and resumed his position stretched out on the mattress with his shoulders propped against a pile of cushions. He tucked his hands behind his head and the action drew Clare's gaze to his bare chest and superb muscle definition.

'So you are not yet absolutely committed to your cause?' he said softly. 'You could change your mind?'

The speculative gleam in his light grey eyes sent a quiver along her spine as she became aware of the sexual chemistry fizzing in the close confines of the Jeep. Clare realised she had swapped one danger for another. She had felt unsafe in the hut, but her intense awareness of Diego could prove to be a greater threat to her peace of mind, especially when his gaze lingered quite blatantly on her breasts that were inadequately covered by her cotton chemise.

She remembered Becky and the vital reason why she needed to get to Torrente. 'Nothing will deter me from the path I have chosen.'

His mouth curved into a sexy smile that should be illegal in front of susceptible females. 'You don't think you could be tempted to choose a different path?'

Heaven help her. She wished he would stop looking at her as if he was imagining stripping her naked and having his wicked way with her. She glanced rather desperately around the Jeep for something to cover herself with. 'Could I borrow a sleeping bag?'

'Help yourself.'

She unzipped the bag and gave it a thorough inspection for tarantulas before she got into it and pulled the zip up to her chin. Immediately her temperature soared but at least her body was hidden from Diego's gaze. 'Temptation is the work of the devil,' she said primly.

'Are you telling me you have never been tempted by desire, which is a perfectly natural human instinct?'

His voice was like molten syrup sliding sensuously over her body, inciting all sorts of shocking images in her head. She was fiercely attracted to Diego but she certainly wasn't going to admit it. 'If I did ever feel tempted…I would pray until those feelings passed.'

The Jeep was suddenly plunged into blackness as Diego switched off the lamp. Clare heard him moving. He was obviously trying to get comfortable but his height meant that he had to lie diagonally across the Jeep.

'While you're praying to be delivered from temptation, maybe you could say one for me, Sister,' he muttered. 'You'd better pray real hard because I keep picturing you in your cotton nightdress and I'll be honest, I've never been so tempted by a woman in my life.'

If the devil *did* exist and was waiting to receive sinners into the fires of hell, he was toast, Diego thought to himself. He was burning up with desire to unzip Sister Clare's sleeping bag and remove the tantalising, almost see-through garment she was wearing. If he had ever given a thought to what nuns wore in bed he would have guessed something demure and ankle-length, not a sexy little slip that left little to his imagination.

'I'm sorry I interrupted you when you were reading,' she said quietly. Her voice was as soft as the velvet darkness surrounding them. 'You told me you had a poor education, so when did you discover an appreciation of classic and contemporary literature? I noticed you have a collection of books by a wide range of authors.'

The question took Diego back almost two decades to when he and Cruz had been employed by Earl Bancroft. His first instinct was to tell Sister Clare to mind her own business, but he needed something to distract his thoughts from his damnable desire for her.

'I once worked at a diamond mine in Brazil which was owned by an English earl. My friend was dating the Earl's daughter, and I used to go to the ranch house with him and chat up the housekeeper.' He grinned. 'Lucia was a few years older than me and she taught me a lot.'

'About literature?' Clare asked disbelievingly.

'Well, no. I admit I was more interested in her physical attributes than her mind. But she used to let me borrow books from the Earl's library while he was away.'

Diego remembered he had been blown away by the number of books to choose from. When he had been in prison, Father Vincenzi had taught him English and encouraged him to read, and he had developed a love of well-written stories—anything from classic literature to political thrillers. After his release he had gone to work at the diamond mine at Montez Claros and had spent his free time in Earl Bancroft's library, glad to escape his life of hard physical labour while he was absorbed in a book.

'What happened to your friend who was dating the Earl's daughter?' Clare asked curiously.

'He married her, eventually, and now they have twin boys.'

'Wouldn't you like to get married like your friend?'

'Nope.'

'Why not?'

Diego gave a contemplative sigh. 'I had a girlfriend once who liked me to buy her boxes of chocolates, but because she was watching her weight she only ate the strawberry creams and left the other flavours. To me, marriage is like only enjoying your favourite chocolate in a selection box and ignoring all the other flavours, which to my way of thinking is a waste,' he explained laconically.

Clare made a choked sound. 'That is the most chauvinistic statement I have ever heard. You are…' she struggled to find an adjective that conveyed her disgust '…*astonishing.*'

'You're not the first woman to think so.'

Clare could not see his expression in the dark Jeep but she pictured his sexy grin. 'I didn't mean it in a good way,' she muttered.

'I still think that how I choose to live my life is more understandable than your decision to deny yourself the pleasures of physical intimacy,' he drawled. 'How can you be certain you won't want to marry in the future if you have never had a relationship with a man? Wouldn't it be a good idea to at least date a few guys before you make your final vows?'

'As a matter of fact I did have a relationship, with a two-timing compulsive liar and cheater.' She could not disguise the bitterness in her voice when she thought of Mark.

'Ah.' Diego's response was laden with meaning.

Clare frowned. 'What do you mean, "Ah"?'

'My theory is that it is possible, likely even, that your decision to become a nun was the result of having your heart broken by the guy who cheated on you.' Diego sounded satisfied that he had resolved a question that had been niggling him. 'You were hurt once and you have decided to hide away from life so that you don't risk getting hurt again.'

Clare was tempted to tell Mr Know-It-All what he could do with his theory but, although she hated to admit it to herself, there *was* a grain of truth in Diego's words. Her break-up with Mark had not made her turn to a religious life, but she had become a bit of a hermit for the past year.

'What was your ex-boyfriend, apart from a jerk? I mean, what job does he do?' Diego reworded his question.

'His name is Mark Penry, which I expect means nothing to you as you spend most of your time living away from civilisation, but he is a very successful male model. He recently appeared in an advertising campaign for the famous Lux brand of underwear. Pictures of Mark wearing just a pair of designer boxer shorts featured on billboards in just about every major city around the world.'

'You mean you broke your heart over a pretty boy who advertises pants?' Diego said sardonically.

'He's not a pretty boy... Well, actually he is,' Clare conceded, remembering how she'd found it irritating when Mark had checked his appearance in every mirror he passed. 'The point is that he let me believe we had a future together. I felt such a fool when I discovered that he was sleeping with another model, especially as many of the other staff at A-Star PR knew, but they didn't tell me because they didn't want to hurt my feelings.'

It was odd that in all other aspects of her life she was sensible to the point of boring, Clare mused, but her good sense seemed to desert her when it came to picking men. She remembered when she was seventeen she'd fallen for a boy at college and had believed Tony returned her feelings. But she'd been devastated when she discovered that he had only asked her out because he'd made a bet with his mates that he could get her into bed. Clare recalled the advice Aunt Edith had given her.

'Don't be in a rush to have sex. One day you will meet the right man, who you will love with all your heart and soul and who will love you.'

Aunt Edith's rather brusque manner had hidden a kind heart. She had understood that Clare had felt second-best when she was a child because her parents had lavished most of their attention on Becky. Clare had taken her aunt's words to heart, and all through university she had dated guys but had never been tempted to take the relationships further. When she'd met Mark she had thought that he was 'the one.' But finding out that he was a liar and cheater had shattered her illusions, especially when Mark had said he'd been forced to get sex elsewhere because of Clare's insistence on waiting until she felt ready to give her virginity to him.

But Mark was a saint compared to Diego Cazorra! She would never be able to look at a box of chocolates again without being reminded of his outrageous attitude towards women. She wished she was brave enough to go and sleep in the hut. It seemed impossible that she would be able to fall asleep when she was supremely conscious of Diego's half-naked body squashed up against her with only her sleeping bag to separate them.

It was her last conscious thought. When she opened her eyes again she saw through the window that the sky had lightened to pearly grey tinged with the palest pink as the sun rose above the tree tops.

Something had disturbed her. She vaguely remembered hearing a harsh voice and realised that Diego was speaking in what she assumed was Portuguese. She unzipped the sleeping bag so that she could sit up, and turned to find him muttering in his sleep. Heaven knew what he was dreaming about. His features were drawn into an expression of terrible anguish and he was tossing his head restlessly from side to side.

'Assassino!' He shouted the word and then covered his face with his forearm and gave a groan that sounded as if it had been ripped from his soul.

'Diego!' She called his name several times but could not wake him. He groaned again as if he was in agony. Was he ill? In desperation, Clare shook his shoulder. 'Diego. Diego. *Mr Cazorra*, wake up.'

He moved so quickly that she was taken off guard when he slid his hand behind her neck and threaded his fingers into her hair.

'Do you remember what I said I would do if you called me Mr Cazorra?' he drawled.

CHAPTER FOUR

DIEGO'S SILVER WOLF'S eyes gleamed with a feral hunger as he drew Clare's face down to his and angled his mouth over her lips. His kiss was like no other she had ever experienced—deeply sensual and so utterly irresistible that she did not stand a chance against his skilful seduction.

Still half-dazed with sleep, but more dazzled by him, her lips parted of their own volition when his mouth exerted subtle pressure. Like a connoisseur of fine wine, he tasted her slowly and unhurriedly, yet with such bone-shaking eroticism that she melted against him.

The sense of unreality she had felt since she'd arrived in Brazil increased, and she sank into a dreamlike state where she was only conscious of the strength of Diego's arms around her, the divine smell of him, and the taste of him when she dipped her tongue into his mouth. He overwhelmed her and the feel of his hand smoothing up and down her spine evoked a languorous warmth in her veins.

It seemed perfectly natural when he rolled her on to her back so that she was lying beneath him. His weight crushed her and she felt the slight abrasion of his chest hairs brush against the upper swell of her breasts above the neckline of her chemise.

He deepened the kiss, and the languorous feeling was replaced with a fierce pull of desire in the pit of her stomach so that she lifted her hips, unconsciously seeking to assuage the ache inside her. She sensed a new urgency in Diego, a barely controlled savagery as he ravished her mouth with his intoxicating mastery, taking everything she offered him and demanding more.

Molten heat pooled between Clare's legs when she felt the hard ridge of Diego's arousal straining beneath his jeans and pushing insistently into the cradle of her hips. She heard him mutter something indistinct and the sexy huskiness in his voice scraped her sensitive nerve endings. He was so *male*, hard against her softness, his passion without frills, without subtlety, a primal hunger that threatened to consume her in its fiery flame.

She lifted her hand and touched the blond stubble on his jaw. It was not rough as she had expected, but felt silky beneath her fingertips. Utterly engrossed, she moved her hand higher to stroke his hair back from his cheek—and froze.

The top of his right ear was missing.

In an instant she was hurtled back to reality as she thought of Becky and the ghastly contents of the box the kidnappers had sent her. Shame engulfed her as she realised that while Diego had been kissing her she had forgotten about her sister's plight.

Diego's jaw hardened when he saw her shocked expression and he flicked his head so that his hair fell forwards to cover his mutilated ear. What did it mean? Clare wondered numbly. Why did he have the same injury that the kidnappers might have inflicted on her sister?

She pushed against his chest and when he rolled off her she snatched a breath and groped for her sanity in a world that had gone mad.

'You were having a nightmare and I was trying to wake you.' She bit her lip as she remembered the indescribable horror in his voice when he'd shouted out. 'What was your dream about? You sounded like you were being tortured.' Her own voice shook and she was incapable of making light of what had happened.

'I don't remember dreaming about anything.' Diego swore silently. He knew what his dream had been about because it was always the same dream. The other inmates had called it the initiation, when new prisoners were beaten until they were a bloodied pulp and the prison guards looked the other way, or sometimes joined in. His horrific nightmares were a legacy of when he had been in prison and, although it was many years since he had been released from what had been a living hell, time had not erased the memories.

'You spoke in your sleep but I couldn't understand

you.' Sister Clare's lovely face looked troubled. 'I wonder if something traumatic happened in your past that you relive in your dreams.'

She was too close to the truth for Diego's comfort. He shrugged. 'You may be right,' he drawled. 'I was deeply traumatised when Brazil lost the football World Cup.'

'I was being serious.' She firmed her lips that moments ago had softened when Diego had kissed her. He dragged his eyes from the temptation of her lush mouth and opened the door of the Jeep, pausing to grab his rucksack containing his wash kit before he jumped down and walked away.

His nightmares were the reason why he had never spent an entire night with a woman before, Diego brooded as he strode through the tribal village. When he visited his mistresses in Rio he always left them after sex and went home to sleep alone. During daytime hours he could control his mind and suppress his memories, but while he slept the demons inside him tortured his subconscious so that sometimes he woke up believing he was back in the prison cell he had shared with ten or more other men. The cell had been so small that the inmates had been forced to take it in turns to lie down on the floor to snatch an hour of sleep if they were lucky.

The experience had left him with an irrational fear of confined spaces which made him come out in a cold sweat whenever he rode in an elevator. Even being in the Jeep sometimes made him feel claustrophobic, and he kept the windows open so that he could feel fresh air on his face. He was sweating now, partly from his nightmare and partly because, as the sun burned through the mist, the humidity in the air rose rapidly. He walked through the trees to where a tributary of the river made a natural pool, which was safe to swim in.

Why the hell had he kissed Sister Clare like that? He had only intended to tease her and brush his lips lightly over hers, but when she had opened her mouth for him and he'd felt her ardent response, he had been powerless to resist her. It had never happened to him before. He was *always* in control.

Diego's jaw clenched. He had just proved that his self-discipline was not infallible and the discovery that he could be tempted to act without restraint shook him badly. If he could succumb to passion, he might just as easily succumb to anger and violence, like he had done when he was seventeen.

He stripped and dived into the pool, relishing the cool water washing over his heated skin. He felt more at home in the rainforest than he did in a city. Here, he was free to live his life on his terms without the need to bow to social conventions. Compared to the *favela* where he had spent his childhood, and prison where he had lost his soul, the tropical wilderness, although dangerous in its own way, provided him with a sense of peace. He would not allow a novice nun with the face of an angel and the body of Aphrodite to disturb his sanctuary, he assured himself.

He looked up at the sky and watched a bank of clouds roll in above the tree tops. Experience told him that another day of heavy rain lay ahead, and flooding would make the road from Inua village up to the border virtually impassable. He shrugged. His task was to escort Sister Clare to Torrente so that she could teach at the Sunday school and prepare to make her final vows and, although he felt she was making a mistake by committing her life to the church, it was her choice and none of his business.

Clare was conscious of Diego's brooding gaze as she stepped out of the guest hut and walked over to where he was leaning against the Jeep. She assumed he had swum in the river as his hair was damp, but it was drying quickly in the stifling heat and turning blonder by the minute. At least he was fully clothed, but his tight-fitting white T-shirt clung to the hard ridges of his abdominal muscles and evoked memories of when she had run her hands over his naked torso.

Although she was too hot in her nun's habit, she was glad that her body was hidden from his view, especially when she felt her hard nipples chafe against her bra. She was shocked by her wanton response to Diego and determined to keep her distance from him for the second leg of their journey to Torrente.

As she drew nearer to him he jammed his hat on to his head and pulled the brim down over his eyes, almost as if he wanted to hide his expression from her. If only her veil offered the same protection, she thought ruefully. A large raindrop landed on the dusty path in front of her, followed by another and another. She glanced up at the sullen clouds that had covered up the sun. 'I'm ready to go. I expect you want to get on the road before the weather worsens.'

She expected him to agree, but he did not move, and her intense awareness of him detected his sudden tension.

'Are you sure you want to continue?' Beneath the brim of his hat his eyes gleamed as bright and hard as polished steel. 'It's not too late for you to change your mind...and choose a different path.'

Clare realised he was not talking about her journey to Torrente. For a split second she was tempted to tell him the truth about why she needed to go to the town, but she could not forget the kidnappers' threat to kill her sister if she involved anyone else. She did not know if she could trust Diego. She barely knew anything about him and the few facts he had divulged about himself made him even more of an enigma.

'I am quite sure of the path I must follow,' she said in a low voice, her throat tightening with fear as she faced the prospect of meeting the kidnappers.

'*Deus*. Just because your boyfriend was a jerk, you are going to cut yourself off from life, from love?' Diego forgot his decision not to get involved in Sister Clare's life. 'When we kissed, you were warm and responsive in my arms. What will you do with all your passion and fire when you are shut away in a convent?'

Clare laughed derisively. 'What do you know about love? A man who describes marriage as limiting himself to choosing only one flavour of chocolates from a selection box?'

He stared at her and then shrugged his shoulders. 'You're right. I've never experienced love.' He opened the door of the Jeep and, before Clare had time to realise his intention, he lifted her off her feet and dumped her on the passenger seat. She took a deep breath to steady her racing heart as he climbed in beside her and started the engine.

'Never?' she asked curiously. 'Didn't your parents love you?'

He did not reply while he negotiated a series of deep holes in the road, but after a few minutes he said, 'I never met my father. He abandoned my mother after he got her pregnant with me. The only information she told me about him was that he was an Englishman called Philip Hawke who had come to work as a travel rep at the hotel in Brazil where my mother was a chambermaid. They had an affair, but when she told him she was expecting his child he returned to England and she never heard from him again.'

But Diego had heard from his father's family. Soon after his release from prison he had been contacted by a law firm in England, who had explained that Philip Hawke had died some years earlier but had confided to his own father that he had an illegitimate child in Brazil. Geoffrey Hawke had spent his remaining years searching for his grandson without success. Before Geoffrey died he had instructed the law firm to continue the search, and eventually they had tracked Diego down and gave him the astounding news that his grandfather had left him a fortune in his will.

The money had allowed Diego to become a business partner with his friend Cruz Delgado. They had bought the Old Betsy diamond mine where Cruz's father had found the famous Estrela Vermelha—the Red Star diamond. The discovery in the mine of diamonds worth millions of dollars—including a rare pink diamond, the Estrela Rosa, which Diego had found and kept in his private collection of gems— had made the two men multimillionaires. Recently, another mine that had been abandoned many years ago and was only discovered when Cruz had been given a map of the hidden tunnels by his father-in-law, Earl Bancroft, had been found to contain a huge supply of diamonds, making Diego and Cruz two of the richest men in Brazil.

Wealth certainly had great benefits, Diego mused. But his penthouse apartment in Rio, his various other properties around the world and even his collection of luxury sports cars were simply toys to amuse him. Nothing filled the void inside him or made him forget the poverty and deprivation of his childhood. When he was growing up, what he had wanted more than anything was to feel loved. Love was more precious than gold or glittering gems but, after thirty-seven years without it, his heart had become as hard and unbreakable as the diamonds he mined.

He forced his thoughts back to the present when he realised Sister Clare was speaking. 'It must have been difficult for your mother to be a single parent. Did you spend your childhood in Manaus?'

'I grew up in a *favela* in the city of Belo Horizonte.' Diego gave a cynical laugh. 'The name translates to beautiful horizon, but there was nothing beautiful about the overcrowded and filthy slum where my mother and I lived.'

'Is that why you like being in the rainforest, because it is wild and beautiful and you can be alone?'

Diego glanced at her. 'I'm not alone now,' he drawled. His gut clenched as he watched rosy colour stain her cheeks. She was so beautiful. But perhaps it was the fact that she was out of bounds that made her all the more desirable. It was one of life's ironies that you always wanted what you couldn't have, he mused.

He was surprised by Sister Clare's perceptiveness, and also how easy he found it to talk to her. He was an expert at chat-up lines, but he rarely talked to women, probably because they rarely listened, he thought sardonically.

'I can breathe in the rainforest,' he admitted. 'There is an honesty here that I have never found anywhere else. It's one of the few places on earth where Mother

Nature is truly untamed, and that makes her fearsome but fascinating.'

He was an instinctive poet, Clare thought. He wove a pattern with words and revealed his love of the rainforest in his gravelly voice. Who was the real Diego Cazorra? So far she had met the loner gold prospector and the notorious womaniser the Mother Superior had warned her about. But she sensed that Diego rarely allowed anyone to see beyond his outward persona of a laid-back, charismatic charmer.

She remembered the book of poems by the English romantic poet John Keats that she had found in the back of the Jeep.

'"To one who has been long in city pent, 'Tis very sweet to look into the fair And open face of heaven— to breathe a prayer Full in the smile of the blue firmament,"' she quoted softly.

Diego glanced at her.

'"Who is more happy, when, with heart's content, Fatigued he sinks into some pleasant lair Of wavy grass, and reads a debonair A gentle tale of love and languishment?"' he finished the quote. 'It seems we have one thing in common, at least. Which other poets do you like, apart from Keats?'

'Oh, Wordsworth, Shelley. I love the work of many of the poets of the late eighteenth century. I am an unashamed romantic at heart. How about you?'

'Am I romantic?' He laughed. 'What do you think, Sister Clare?'

'I think you are more than a tough gold prospector.' She hesitated, then felt compelled to ask, 'What happened to your ear?'

'An accident,' he said abruptly. Instantly the connection between them was severed. Clare wished she had suppressed her curiosity, but it was too late to withdraw her question and Diego's answer revealed nothing. She could not tell him her interest was not nosiness, but that she carried with her a box containing what was very possibly a piece of her sister's ear, cut off by the criminals who had kidnapped Becky.

She had only glimpsed Diego's ear, but it had been enough time for her to notice that the top half appeared to have been sliced off. The skin had healed over, as if the injury had not happened recently. Clare had read that a common tactic used by gangs in Brazil to scare families into paying a ransom for their kidnapped relatives was to send them a piece of the victim's ear. There were even cosmetic surgeons who specialised in rebuilding mutilated ears. But Diego had told her that he had grown up in a slum after his father had abandoned his mother, and it seemed unlikely that he had been kidnapped and a ransom demanded for his release.

The mystery surrounding him grew ever deeper. She glanced at him as he concentrated on steering the Jeep around the potholes in the road. He had tipped his hat forwards so that the brim hid his expression, and she sensed that the barriers he had briefly lowered were back in place.

* * *

The rain did not stop after an hour or so as it had the previous day, but continued to fall in a relentless torrent that turned the dirt road into a muddy river. Clare lost count of the number of times the Jeep became stuck and she had to get out and help Diego free the wheels from the ochre-coloured soup. By late afternoon she was so tired that she moved on autopilot as she aided him in laying wooden planks beneath the Jeep's front wheels. Diego climbed into the driver's seat and accelerated until slowly, slowly the vehicle inched forwards. He drove into a small clearing in the trees where the ground was covered in a tangle of creeping vines and watched Clare trudge towards him.

'I'll say this, Sister. You are one determined lady.' There was admiration in his voice. 'Most people would have given up by now and asked to turn back, but I haven't heard you complain once about the rain and the damned mud.' He felt a flicker of something that could have been tenderness as he watched her valiantly try to haul herself into the Jeep. She was so tired she could hardly lift her foot on to the step and she did not protest when he lifted her up and deposited her on the seat.

Clare gave him a weary smile. 'I *will* get to Torrente, whatever it takes. A bit of mud won't stop me.'

She leaned her head against the back of the seat and closed her eyes, giving Diego an opportunity to study her without her being aware of his intent scrutiny. Her nun's habit and veil were rain-soaked and her shoes and legs were covered in mud. She was pale with exhaustion so that the golden freckles scattered across her nose and cheeks were noticeable against her creamy complexion.

Desire, as inexplicable as it was inconvenient, tugged in Diego's gut. He liked leggy blondes whose sexual experience matched his own, and he could not understand why it took all his will power to resist covering Sister Clare's mouth with his lips and kissing her until she responded as passionately as she had when he had kissed her that morning.

She lifted her lashes, and Diego stared into the deep blue pools of her eyes. *Deus*, why did he feel an urge to open his heart to her and tell her things about himself that he had never revealed to anyone else?

Cursing his stupidity beneath his breath, he restarted the engine and drove back to the road. 'The rain is easing up and I reckon we'll get to Torrente in a couple more hours.'

When they reached the town he would leave her at the church and never see her again. She had chosen a way of life that prevented her from having a relationship with a man. And he had to face it, Diego mocked himself, he could not have offered her a relationship. All he wanted was to have sex with her, and once he had sated his desire he would no doubt have grown bored of her as quickly as he did with all his mistresses.

'Do you know of a big waterfall near to Torrente?'

He nodded. 'Branco Cachoeirao. The waterfall is three or four miles outside the town.'

'I believe there is a cave nearby, and inside there is a shrine to the Virgin Mary which was carved out of rock by a missionary who was one of the first non-indigenous people to visit Torrente many years ago.'

Diego shrugged. 'I was unaware of a shrine, but I know the cave you mean.'

'Good, because I would like you to take me to it before you drive on to the town. I want to spend the night alone at the shrine in quiet contemplation—' Clare's voice faltered '—and I'll make my own way to Torrente tomorrow.'

'Let me get this straight. You want me to leave you on your own in the rainforest for the night? Sister, you are either crazily brave or just crazy.' Diego shot a glance at her serene face and was tempted to shake some sense into her. He could not comprehend why she was willing to sacrifice her passionate nature for a life of austerity and physical denial, but he was convinced that her broken relationship with her ex-boyfriend who had cheated on her had influenced her decision to become a nun.

The rain finally stopped, which made the driving conditions easier, and as they drew closer to Torrente Diego reminded himself that Clare's decision had nothing to do with him. His gut told him she needed to be saved from making a mistake, but his mind pointed out that he was not the man to save her.

* * *

Clare heard the waterfall before she saw it. The thunderous noise of the falls drowned out the sounds of the rainforest that she was starting to recognise: the various calls of hundreds of species of birds, the chatter and shrieks of monkeys and occasionally a deep roar that Diego had told her was a jaguar.

He steered the Jeep down a narrow track where light could barely penetrate through the tangle of trees and vines that formed a living green roof. They emerged into a clearing, and in front was a spectacular sight of white frothing water plunging hundreds of feet over rocks into the river below.

'If I remember rightly, the cave is further on.' Diego inched the Jeep slowly through the dense forest, past giant ferns and plants with leaves that Clare estimated were two metres or more in diameter. A huge cliff of grey rock towered so high that she had to tilt her head to see the top. She peered through the eerie gloom of the jungle and saw a black hole in the rocks. The entrance to the cave was overgrown with vegetation, as if no humans had visited the place for a long time.

Diego stopped the Jeep and jumped out. Clare followed him and gave a startled cry when a wild boar raced out of the cave and disappeared into the undergrowth.

'Do you really intend to spend the night in there?' he asked sardonically as she lingered outside the cave. He obviously sensed her reluctance to step into the blackness. Swallowing hard, she switched on her torch and directed its beam into the dark space before she walked slowly forwards.

'Do you think there could be any other animals in here?' Her voice echoed as it bounced off the cave walls.

'You might find a rock python.'

'Funny,' she muttered, telling herself he was joking. Pythons didn't live in caves, did they? The light from the torch flickered over something that caught her attention. Heart pounding, she moved deeper into the cave and drew a sharp breath when she saw a face. It was not a real person, she quickly realised, but a statue of the Virgin Mary that had been carved into a rock. The figure was about three feet tall and exquisitely detailed, just as the Mother Superior had described it.

There was something incredibly moving about the statue that a priest had painstakingly carved out of the solid rock a century earlier. It must have taken him months to complete and must have been a true labour of devotion. Clare could not explain why a feeling of calm came over her as she touched the figure of Mary, but her tiredness was replaced with a sense of optimism that she would be able to rescue Becky.

She stood by the statue for some time until she became aware of something moving on a rock close to her. She shone the torch in the direction of the rustling sound, and in the light she saw the glint of greeny-brown scales.

Dear heaven, Diego hadn't been joking! Giving a scream loud enough to wake the dead, she ran towards the cave entrance and collided full pelt into him.

'Easy, Sister.' Diego took one look at her white face and, fearing she was about to faint, gripped her by her elbows and held her upright. 'I'm guessing you saw a snake?' When she nodded he said gently, 'Wait here and I'll get rid of it.'

Clare had no intention of following him into the cave and she looked away with a shudder when he walked past her holding a long green snake in his hands. He carried the reptile away from the entrance and came back a few minutes later with some logs and dry twigs that he must have collected from the forest floor.

'What are you doing?'

'Building a fire. It'll burn throughout the night and keep unwanted visitors out of the cave.'

'What about the creatures that have already taken up residence?' Clare gave another shudder as she pictured the python Diego had evicted.

'I took a look around and saw nothing else in the cave. But there is a hole in the roof, which is lucky.'

'Lucky, how? If it rains I'll get wet.'

'It's only a small hole, but rainwater has poured in and made a pool of fresh water that you can drink.' Diego noticed she was still pale from her fright with the python and her eyes looked like dark bruises in her white face. 'Why don't you go and splash some water on your face and freshen up while I get your bags from the Jeep?'

Clare held her torch tightly in her trembling hand and forced herself to walk to the back of the cave. She *had* to spend the night here for Becky's sake, she reminded herself. The kidnappers had instructed her to be at the cave on Sunday but they had not specified at what time. They might arrive at dawn and she could not risk missing them, hence her decision to stay in the rainforest overnight, although she was certain she would not sleep at all. Her nerves were at breaking point but she dared not ask Diego to stay with her in case he was seen by the kidnappers.

She found the small pool where a natural basin that had formed in the rocks had filled with rainwater, and felt marginally better once she had washed her face. But the prospect of meeting the kidnappers the next day filled her with dread. Was Becky still alive? What if the kidnappers took the ransom money and killed both of them? Before she had left England her sister's kidnapping had seemed surreal, but now the danger of the situation was terrifyingly immediate.

A golden glow suddenly flared at the front of the cave and she saw that Diego had lit the fire and also the kerosene lamp, which he had brought from the Jeep. He had been busy, and Clare's heart clenched when she saw that he had spread a sleeping bag on the floor and brought in a few cushions to make her makeshift bed as comfortable as possible.

He glanced at her. 'Sleep close to the fire and you'll be safe from any curious forest creatures. I've brought your bags from the Jeep and also some dried fruit and nuts for breakfast.'

'Thank you.' His gruff concern brought tears to her eyes. 'You are very kind.'

He was standing on the opposite side of the fire to her and his muscular body was silhouetted against the darkening sky outside the cave. His face was shadowed by the brim of his hat but Clare saw the gleam of his white teeth when he grinned. 'I'm no saint, Sister.'

'Perhaps not, but I think you are a better man than you know,' she said seriously.

For several moments he stared at her across the flames that danced between them before he turned abruptly and walked out of the cave, disappearing into the dusk. Seconds later Clare heard the sound of the Jeep's engine, and only then did reality hit her that he had left without saying goodbye and she was alone in the rainforest.

It was what she had planned, she reminded herself. It was vital that Diego was not around when she met the kidnappers tomorrow. So why did she feel numb inside? Why did she feel as if her heart had been torn from her chest? He was a womaniser who made Mark look like boyfriend of the year. But he was also courageous—she remembered how he had captured the python. During the long and arduous journey from Manaus he had proved himself to be patient and dependable, and he had even poured away his beer when she had told him about Aunt Edith being killed by a drunk driver.

The tears she'd managed to hold back before Diego had left now spilled over. She was tired and scared and, to make matters worse, as she huddled close to the fire her damp clothes began to steam. It seemed sensible to at least attempt to sleep, and so she took off the nun's habit and veil and spread them on a rock, hoping they would dry before she had to put them on in the morning.

It was too hot next to the fire for her to get into the sleeping bag but she rearranged the cushions Diego had given her and discovered that he had left behind the book of Keats's poems. His kind gesture undid her completely and she choked back a sob. She felt utterly alone, but a faint noise from outside the cave put her senses on high alert. She strained her ears, hardly daring to breathe. Something or someone was out there and she did not know if she would prefer the intruder to be a wild animal or a kidnapper.

The unmistakable crunch of boots on the gravel floor at the cave's entrance escalated Clare's terror. Her instinct was to hide but she firmed her jaw, determined not to give in to her fear. If the men who had kidnapped her sister were here it was up to her to deal with them. For Becky's sake she must be brave.

She stood up and hurriedly wrapped the sleeping bag around her. *'Who's there?'*

'It's me, of course.' Diego strolled into the cave and the light from the fire illuminated his big frame. 'Who did you think it could be? No one else is mad enough to spend a night in the jungle.' He threw his sleeping bag down on the floor and tossed his hat on to a rock before raking his fingers through his hair that for some reason was wet although it was not raining outside.

Clare stared at him, hardly able to believe he was real and not a figment of her imagination. He had changed into clean jeans and a denim shirt that was unbuttoned to halfway down his chest, and he looked so ruggedly gorgeous that her heart rate rocketed.

'I…I heard the Jeep and I thought you had driven on to Torrente,' she stammered.

'I noticed the wheels were sinking into the mud, so I moved the Jeep to firmer ground and then took a shower beneath the waterfall.' He stepped around the fire and frowned when he saw tears on her cheeks. 'You didn't really think I would abandon you in the rainforest, did you?'

His sexy smile shattered Clare's tenuous hold on her composure. The terror she had felt a few minutes ago had been needless. Diego was here and for now at least she felt safe. The sleeping bag fell from her shoulders as she gave an inarticulate cry and flew across the few feet separating them to launch herself at his chest.

'I thought you had gone and I would never see you again.' It was a sign of her emotional state that she did not consider how betraying her words were. All she cared about was that Diego had appeared, tall and strong, like a blond Viking. His bare skin revealed by his half-open shirt felt warm beneath her hands as she clung to him.

'Clare?' His voice was deeper than she had ever heard it as his arms came round her and enfolded her. He hesitated for a fraction of a second before he lifted her off her feet and crushed her to him. '*Deus*, do you think I could bear to leave you, *anjinho*?' he murmured against her lips before he claimed her mouth in a searing kiss that plundered her soul.

CHAPTER FIVE

DIEGO BRIEFLY FOUGHT and lost a battle with his conscience. A saint would not be able to resist Clare's
passionate response, he told himself, feeling his erection strain against the constriction of his jeans as she
parted her lips beneath his.

He was surprised to discover a vulnerable side
to her. On the journey from Manaus he had been
impressed by her determined spirit and amused by
her dry sense of humour. But now she was clearly
distraught and he felt her tremble as she burrowed
against him like a frightened animal seeking shelter from danger.

She was so tiny. He felt a surge of protectiveness.
'What's the matter, *pequeno*?' Instinctively he felt
sure that her tears were not just because she had believed he'd left her alone at the cave.

'I don't know if I am doing the right thing.' Clare's
iron control over her nerves crumbled and her fears
poured out in a flood of tears. Maybe she should have
gone to the police and asked them to find her sister's

kidnappers. Maybe she wasn't brave but stupid and naïve to think that she could rescue Becky.

'It's natural for you to have doubts,' Diego said gently as understanding dawned in him. Clare was facing the biggest decision of her life when she would make her final vows and commit herself fully to a nun's life. Perhaps she was having second thoughts about the life she had chosen. His conscience told him he should step away from her and suppress his desire, somehow stifle the sexual chemistry that existed between them, which must add to her confusion about her future. But how could he resist her when she wound her arms around his neck and sought his mouth with hers, initiating a sensual kiss that stirred his body into urgent awareness?

She did not look like a nun. When he had walked into the cave and seen her wearing just a plain white bra and knickers, with her auburn curls tumbling around her shoulders, he'd been stunned by her beauty. She was a petite package of voluptuous curves and he could not stop himself from running his hands over her body, exploring the gentle flare of her hips and the indent of her slender waist.

She tensed when he slid his hands across her ribcage and lightly stroked his fingers over the underside of her breasts. But she did not pull her mouth away from his, and when he deepened the kiss she melted into him and parted her lips to allow him to push his tongue between them.

Diego heard a faint voice inside his head warning

him that he must not take advantage of her innocent eagerness. But she had told him she'd had one serious relationship, he reminded himself, so she could not be completely innocent. The way she was kissing him with fiery passion and sliding her hands over his chest was heating his blood and evoking a primal hunger in him that obliterated all rational thoughts from his mind and left only an insistent throb of desire that demanded to be appeased.

Once again, the situation Clare found herself in seemed surreal. A week ago she had been engrossed in company spreadsheets and wondering what to wear to the Association of Accountants' Christmas dinner. Now she was in a cave in the Amazon rainforest, dreading tomorrow when she would meet her sister's kidnappers, but at this moment she was half-naked and the sexiest man on the planet had laid her down on a sleeping bag and was looking at her with a gleam in his eyes that blazed hotter than the flames of the fire.

Maybe it was all a dream, and if so she did not want to wake up from this part of it. The sensible, circumspect Clare Marchant from England had been transformed by the sultry heat of the Brazilian rainforest into a sensual siren who was burning up with desire. Diego incited in her a need for sexual fulfilment that she had never felt with any other man.

She realised she had been fooling herself by thinking that her decision not to sleep with Mark was because she had wanted to be sure of their relationship. He seemed like a preening, self-obsessed boy compared to Diego's raw masculinity, and the truth was that Mark had not turned her on like Diego did. She had been unaware until now that she was capable of feeling such an intensity of lust. Every word of Aunt Edith's advice about waiting to fall in love before she gave away her virginity was drowned out by the loud drumbeat of desire pounding through her veins.

Diego was kneeling above her, his thighs straddling her hips and his hands resting on the ground on either side of her head so that she was caged by his powerful body. In the firelight his blond hair looked like a golden halo, but he was a fallen angel with a wicked promise in his eyes to fulfil Clare's wildest fantasies.

He bent his head and kissed her mouth again, slower this time, coaxing her lips open so that he could take his pleasure while he increased hers until she moaned softly and curved her arms around his neck. His blatant seduction intoxicated her senses and made her want more, more…

She snatched air into her lungs when he finally released her mouth and trailed his lips down her throat, but the sensation of him sucking the tender skin at the base of her neck where a pulse beat erratically made her catch her breath. The caress was outrageously erotic, but he did not give her time to assimilate the new sensations he was creating, for he was already sliding his lips lower, over the slope of one breast.

Clare felt his warm breath through the material of her bra cup and wished his mouth was on her bare skin. He must have read her thoughts because he slipped his hand beneath her back and, with a deftness that indicated plenty of experience in undressing women, unfastened the clasp and removed her bra.

His silver wolf's eyes gleamed as he rested back on his haunches and stared at her naked breasts. Clare had always felt self-conscious of her curvaceous shape and compared herself unfavourably to her sister who was a model-thin size zero. But the undisguised hunger in Diego's eyes made her glad that her breasts were full and firm, and for the first time in her life she felt proud of her feminine figure.

She did not feel apprehensive when she read the feral intent in his gaze. She felt as though she had been waiting for this, for *him* all her life. Sexual chemistry had sizzled from the moment they'd met and she felt a connection with him on a fundamental level that defied explanation.

'Diego…' She whispered his name like a prayer.

He gave her an oddly crooked smile and held his finger over her lips. 'Don't speak, *anjinho*. Maybe this isn't real, and I don't want to return to reality,' he said softly.

Clare understood exactly what he meant. It was easy to sink into the dream and forget the world beyond the fire-lit cave; easy to sink into bliss as Diego lifted his finger from her lips and traced a feather-light path down her throat to her breast. She sucked in a sharp breath when he touched her nipple and it immediately hardened.

His husky laugh was rough with desire. *'Bela.'* He was still kneeling above her and he cradled her breasts in his hands and flicked his thumb pads across her nipples in a repetitive motion that created such a storm of exquisite sensations in Clare that the pleasure was almost too much to withstand. Diego lowered his blond head and soothed one engorged peak with his tongue before he drew it into his mouth and suckled her until she moaned, and he transferred his lips to her other nipple and lavished the same delicious torment.

She tangled her fingers in his hair and tugged to bring his face close to hers. His smile should come with a government health warning, she thought, but then he claimed her lips in a possessive kiss that emptied her mind of all rational thoughts and left only the certainty that she wanted the kiss to last for ever.

His passion was scorching, yet he tempered his hunger with an unexpected tenderness that infiltrated her heart. When he slipped his hand between her legs it felt perfectly natural for him to caress the silken skin of her inner thighs. Clare's lack of experience meant that this was uncharted territory for her, but she offered no resistance as his fingers skimmed inexorably higher and slipped inside her knickers.

'Open your legs for me, *querida*. That's right,' he murmured his approval when she relaxed her thighs to allow him to gently part her and he discovered the slick wetness of her arousal. The first probing touch of his finger gently easing into her was enough to almost send her over the edge. Her body quivered but instinct told her to try to control the pulsing sensation deep in her core because it was only the start of a journey that she wanted to take with Diego.

To distract herself from her body's response to him she concentrated on his body and undid the last few buttons so that she could pull off his shirt. He had an incredible muscular physique. In the firelight, the satiny skin on his shoulders gleamed like bronze and the hairs covering his chest were pure gold. She ran her hands down over his flat abdomen to the fuzz of hairs visible above his jeans and, after a second's hesitation, she undid the button on the waistband. Her forwardness would have shocked her if she hadn't been in a dreamlike state where anything was possible and nothing was shocking.

He kissed her breasts again, teased each swollen nipple in turn until she moaned and jerked her hips towards the heat and hardness of him in an unconscious betrayal of her need. The gossamer-soft brush of his lips over her stomach elicited a molten warmth between her legs, and when he kissed her *there*, where no other man had ever touched her before, and when she felt his tongue flick across her clitoris, she could not control the pulse waves of pleasure as her body juddered in a swift, intense climax.

She was spinning out of control. It felt as if she was riding a carousel and images and sensations were flashing past her faster and faster. She did not remember when Diego had removed her knickers or the rest of his clothes, and when he stretched out next to her and drew her against his naked body she was too absorbed in sliding her hands over his impressive abdominal muscles to care. He was a work of art and she delighted in tracing her fingertips down his flat stomach and powerful thighs until she came into contact with the solid length of his erection. Her breath left her lungs in a whoosh. He felt big and hard in her hand and she was curious to know what he would feel like inside her.

When she stretched her fingers around him he gave a low groan of primitive sexual need that stirred an equally primitive response in her. He lifted himself over her and it felt perfectly natural to guide the tip of his swollen shaft towards her moist opening. Instinctively she spread her legs wider to allow him to settle his hips between hers, and he slowly eased forwards, entering her inch by careful inch until he possessed her utterly.

Clare caught her breath as she experienced a moment of mild discomfort, but the brief stinging sensation was over before she really registered it. Diego hesitated, but she curved her arms around his back and pulled him down on to her at the same time as she lifted her hips in invitation for him to take her virginity that she offered willingly.

He waited until her breathing had steadied before he moved, slowly at first, pulling back so far that she thought he was actually going to withdraw. He laughed softly when she clutched his shoulders, and pushed forwards again, then drew back, then forwards, increasing his pace with each thrust and going deeper into her so that she was filled by him, overwhelmed by him and felt that he had taken ownership of her body.

In this primal dance of sex he was her master and her tutor. He slid his hands beneath her bottom and tilted her hips, forcing her to accept each devastating thrust of his body into hers. But he countered his strength with gentleness and there was no question of him forcing her to do anything she did not feel ready to experience. She wanted everything he gave her, wanted more, wanted quite desperately the something that hovered frustratingly just out of her reach.

'Easy, *querida*,' his deep voice soothed her. 'Don't be in such a rush. Relax and let it happen.'

She looked into his eyes and saw a familiar glint of amusement at her impatience. But as she watched him make love to her she saw heat and hunger in his predatory wolf's gaze, and she heard the hoarse sound of his breaths coming faster and faster as he increased his pace.

And then it did happen. Suddenly. Spectacularly.

He gave a powerful thrust that made her gasp, but before she could drag oxygen into her lungs, the tight knot of tension deep in her pelvis exploded without warning and sent her soaring and sobbing into the stratosphere. Her vaginal muscles contracted and re-leased as wave after wave of intense pleasure swept over her so that she could not breathe or think, could only feel the shattering ecstasy of her orgasm.

Diego waited until she came down before he im-mediately took her higher again, driving into her with an implacable intent that made her realise he was nearing his own nirvana. She let him ride her fast and hard, instinctively knowing that he needed it like this and the time for gentleness had passed. His passion was raw and elemental. But when he paused and tipped his head back so that the cords on his neck stood out, before giving a harsh groan that sounded as though it had been torn from his soul, Clare was overcome with tenderness for him and pressed her face against his shoulder to hide the tears that inex-plicably filled her eyes.

Diego pushed his hat off his face where he'd placed it over his eyes before he'd fallen asleep and was instantly aware of three things. The fire had gone out, the slice of sky that he could see through the cave's entrance was a couple of shades lighter than pitch-black and Sister Clare was lying beside him, as naked as the day she'd been born and, fortunately, fast asleep.

Santa Mãe! He'd found himself in some awkward situations in his life, mostly after he'd drunk more beer than was good for him. But he doubted that all the saints in heaven could help him out of this one. His eyes dropped to the delectable curves of Clare's buttocks and he cursed softly beneath his breath and pulled the sleeping bag over her.

There was no point wasting time in recriminations. He couldn't despise himself any more than he already did anyway, and deflowering a nun simply added another black mark against his name. An image came into his head of the overcrowded prison cell where he had spent two years of his life. His mind flashed back further. He saw the figure of a man sprawled on the floor of his mother's apartment, and a pool of black congealed blood.

Diego swallowed convulsively and forced himself to look at his hands. There was no blood on them now. He breathed easier. Of course there wasn't; he only saw the blood in his dreams. It had been years ago, and Father Vincenzi had said he hadn't killed the guy. But how could the priest know for sure, Diego brooded, if he had no recollection himself of what had happened the night he had found his mother being beaten up by a drug dealer? The only person who knew the truth was his mother, but the last time he had seen her he'd been seventeen, and she had told the police he was a murderer.

Deus. He snapped a shutter down on his memories and quickly pulled on his jeans, taking care not to disturb Clare. She looked angelic as she slept with her lips slightly parted and her auburn curls spread across her shoulders. But, thanks to him, she was no longer innocent. After she'd mentioned an ex-boyfriend, he had assumed that she wasn't a virgin, and by the time he had discovered her inexperience, he'd been unable to stop himself from making love to her.

Other memories assailed him, not of the distant past but the previous night. He visualised Clare's curvaceous body, her round, creamy breasts topped with pointed, cherry-red nipples that had been ripe for his mouth. The taste of her still lingered on his lips from when he'd kissed her between her thighs and dipped his tongue into the honeydew of her arousal.

He swore beneath his breath and walked out of the cave before he succumbed to the temptation to kiss her awake and instigate an early morning ride. It would be a first for him because he had never spent an entire night with a woman to be able to have sex upon waking. It was curious that he had slept dreamlessly with Clare cuddled up against him, her body all soft and warm like a kitten, he mused. But he had a feeling that in the cold light of day his little cat would reveal her sharp claws and accuse him of seducing her.

Because undoubtedly, and not entirely unfairly, Clare was going to blame him for leading her astray from the life of pious devotion she had chosen. She was unlikely to believe he hadn't intended for things to go so far. But it wasn't all his fault, Diego tried to convince himself. The way she had thrown herself into his arms would have tested a saint, let alone a mortal man.

He tried to dismiss the voice in his head, which said that he should have been stronger and given Clare time to decide if she wanted to give up her life with the church and give her virginity to him. Instead he had lost control and made love to her mindlessly and without a care for the consequences, and it was that which concerned him more than anything else. No other woman had ever made him feel as desperate for sex as Clare had done last night. He didn't do desperate or, God help him, needy. He was a lone wolf without cares or commitments as far as his numerous temporary mistresses were concerned. It was better that way. Safer.

The sky was lightening with the arrival of dawn as Diego followed the path through the trees towards where he had left the Jeep. He rubbed a hand over his rough jaw and decided he needed a shave. Maybe taking a shower beneath the powerful waterfall would help him to think straight and answer a vital question: *What the hell was he going to do with Clare now?*

The answer slipped unexpectedly easily into his head. He would have to take her back to Rio with him. He felt partly responsible that, now that they had slept together, she could not make her final vows to become a nun. But really he had done her a favour. Her uninhibited response to him last night proved she wasn't cut out for a life of chastity. He would set her up in an apartment near to his penthouse over-looking Copacabana beach, and then he would take her shopping. He was looking forward to seeing her dressed in sexy clothes that made the most of her gorgeous figure, instead of her drab grey nun's habit.

His erotic fantasy of watching Clare parade around his bedroom wearing a see-through black negligee came to an abrupt halt when he heard a noise that instantly put him on his guard. The snap of a twig on the floor of the rainforest could have been made by an animal, but Diego knew that only humans moved so clumsily.

He jerked his head in the direction of the noise and saw the dull silver gleam of a gun aimed at him through the trees. His first instinct was to warn Clare she was in imminent danger but, as he gave a shout, he felt something hard hit his skull, followed by sear-ing pain and nothing more.

She hurt everywhere, Clare discovered when she stretched and became aware of a slight soreness be-tween her legs. Her back ached from where she had spent the night lying on the hard floor of the cave and, when she sat up, internal muscles she had never felt before twinged, and she winced as the zip of the sleeping bag grazed her acutely sensitive nipples.

Glancing down, she saw the swollen reddened tips of her breasts and felt a mixture of shame at the memory of her wanton behaviour, coupled with a newly awakened awareness of her sexual needs. Diego had satisfied her last night, but now she felt ready to play again. It seemed that her body was determined to make up for being a late starter in experiencing sensual pleasure.

It was immediately apparent that she was alone. Diego must have dressed—his jeans and shirt were missing—and only her bra and knickers were strewn on the floor where he had thrown them after he had removed them with her willing cooperation.

The pale pink sky outside the cave reassured her that it must be early morning and thankfully it seemed that the kidnappers had not yet arrived. Fear sent a cold chill down her spine and self-disgust churned in her stomach. While she had made love with Diego, Becky had spent another night in terror, held prisoner by the criminal gang who had snatched her.

Feeling guilty that she had temporarily forgotten about her sister, Clare stood up and pulled on her nun's habit, before covering her hair with the veil. Of course she would explain to Diego that she wasn't really a nun and also explain about Becky being kidnapped. He would probably argue when she asked him to leave her alone at the cave, but to save her sister's life she must follow the kidnappers' instructions and meet them on her own.

She picked up her rucksack and the case of money and stepped outside, but there was no sign of Diego or the Jeep. She vaguely remembered that she had been woken by what had sounded like a shout. Unease made her skin prickle. Where was he? She was about to call him, but hesitated. The forest was eerily silent without the usual cacophony of birdsong, and she sensed that she was being watched.

'Senhorita Marchant?'

A man stepped out from the trees to one side of Clare. She whirled round to face him and inhaled sharply when she saw he was holding a gun. He, and the two men who followed him into the clearing, looked of Hispanic origin, dark-eyed and swarthy-skinned, with an air of menace about them that filled her with dread as she imagined them hurting her sister.

'Where's Becky?'

The man with the gun seemed to be transfixed by her habit and veil. He glanced at the briefcase. 'You have the money?' When she nodded, he held out his hand for her to give him the case.

'I want to see Becky first.' Clare could feel her heart thumping painfully hard in her chest. She had never thought of herself as particularly brave. But her bravery had never been tested when she had lived an ordinary, unexciting life in a leafy north London suburb, she acknowledged. She pictured her father, waiting desperately for news of his daughters, and her fragile mother who was struggling to regain her health after suffering a stroke. Her parents would be devastated if Becky did not return home and Clare knew she was the only person who could secure her sister's release.

She curled her fingers tightly around the handle of the briefcase and stared unflinchingly at the kidnapper when he pointed the gun at her. For some reason she remembered Diego's admiration when she had ignored her exhaustion and helped him dig the Jeep's wheels out of the mud on the road to Torrente. He had made her feel like she was stronger and capable of achieving more than she'd ever realised. Her heart lurched as she wondered where he was and prayed he was safe.

It took all her will power to prevent her hand from shaking as she reached out and calmly pushed the gun away so that it was no longer aimed at her. 'Would you really shoot a nun?'

To her surprise and relief, the kidnapper lowered the weapon to his side and a dull flush mottled his face. 'My apologies, Sister. I was sent here to collect a ransom. I did not realise I would be meeting *uma noiva de Cristo.*'

Clare silently thanked the Mother Superior, who had persuaded her to dress as a nun for her protection. 'I will pay the ransom when my sister is released and transport has been arranged for us to return to England.'

The man shrugged. 'You must come with us,' he said, pointing through the trees to a four-by-four with blacked-out windows parked near the road. He looked at Clare and made the sign of a cross. 'I am sorry, Sister, I just do my job.'

* * *

Torrente looked as deprived and rundown as Diego had described it. The main road was busy with street traders selling their goods from the back of carts, and barefoot children played in the piles of rubbish heaped in the gutters. There was an air of despair about the place, and Clare noticed several young women—some did not look much older than girls—dressed in revealing dresses and towering heels, trying to attract the attention of men who were willing to pay for sex.

The kidnapper who Clare had overheard his companions call Enzo drove through the town and turned up a winding road leading to a huge villa that stood on top of a hill. Whoever lived here was certainly not poor, she thought, as electric gates opened to allow the four-by-four to pass through and closed with an ominous clang behind them. The lush, beautifully manicured grounds were patrolled by armed security guards, and the guards at the front door looked at her closely as she followed Enzo inside.

She had a vague impression of gleaming white marble walls and flashy gold decor, but her heart was beating so fast with fear that she was finding it hard to breathe. They walked along what seemed like miles of corridors before Enzo stopped and opened a door, indicating for Clare to enter the room. She stepped inside and her legs almost buckled with relief when a familiar figure jumped up from a chair and ran towards her.

'Becky!' Clare flew across the room and flung her arms around her sister. 'Are you all right? They haven't harmed you?' Another wave of relief surged through her when she saw that Becky's ears, revealed where her long ash-blonde hair was tied back in a ponytail, were perfectly fine. Clare wondered briefly who the severed piece of ear she had been sent by the kidnappers belonged to. But, thankfully, her sister seemed to be unhurt, and in fact looked as beautiful and elegant as she always did, despite having been held captive for a week.

Compared to Becky, Clare knew she must look like a grubby urchin from a Dickensian novel in her crumpled, mud-stained clothes. She realised that her sister was staring at her veil.

'Why are you dressed like that?' Becky pulled the veil from Clare's head and watched her hair tumble around her shoulders. 'Thank goodness you haven't cut your hair short. It's your best feature.'

'It was a disguise. I was helped by some nuns in Manaus and the Mother Superior suggested that I should wear a habit and veil as protection from the criminals in Torrente who are apparently God-fearing, although they don't fear the police.'

Becky gave a shaky laugh. 'I thought for a minute you had actually joined the church. Wearing the veil makes you look like a very realistic nun.' She glanced across the sitting room to a door which led into an adjoining room. 'Don't you think so, Diego?'

Shock robbed Clare of the ability to speak as she

spun round and stared at Diego leaning against the door frame, his arms folded across his broad chest and his lips curved into a familiar cynical smile that was not reflected in his hard as steel eyes. 'You certainly convinced me, *Sister* Clare,' he drawled.

CHAPTER SIX

'I WAS GOING to tell you, but I didn't get an opportunity to explain,' Clare muttered. She and Diego were walking along a corridor, following the gang member Enzo, who had ordered them to go with him. Clare hadn't had a chance to replace her veil, and she felt vulnerable now that her guise of a nun had been blown. The way Enzo's eyes had insolently roamed over her made her skin crawl.

She wondered if the person called Rigo, who they were being taken to, was the leader of the kidnappers. She was worried that she'd had to leave Becky in the room where they had briefly been reunited. But hopefully this Rigo would accept the ransom money and allow her and Becky, and Diego, to go free, she told herself.

Diego shot her a scathing glance. 'We had sex, and it wasn't a quickie, over in a couple of minutes. How much *more* of an opportunity did you need to mention that you were only pretending to be a nun?'

He swore with muted savagery, aware that their

captor walking just ahead of them could overhear. 'Do you know what a bad time my conscience gave me when I discovered you were…a virgin?' he said harshly.

He was furious with her for making him feel a fool, although her air of innocence hadn't all been an act, he brooded, remembering how she had gasped at the moment of penetration, making him realise, too late, that it was her first time.

'Is that why you had disappeared when I woke up this morning? You felt guilty, so you cleared off.' Clare's initial feeling of relief that Diego had gone from the cave when the kidnappers arrived had gradually turned to anger that he hadn't even woken her to say thanks for their one-night stand, which, of course, was all he had wanted from her.

'I didn't clear off. I was on my way to the waterfall to take a shower when I was ambushed and knocked unconscious.' Diego removed his hat that he'd been wearing with the brim pulled low over his eyes, and Clare made a choked sound when she saw a purple lump on his temple.

'I'm sorry you've been involved. A week ago my sister was snatched while she was on a modelling assignment in Rio, and the kidnappers demanded a ransom for her release. I was instructed to take the money to a cave by a waterfall near to Torrente and was warned that if I went to the police or asked anyone for help Becky would be killed.'

'You should have told me what you were doing.'

'I didn't know if I could trust you.'

'If you didn't trust me, why did you give your-self to me?'

Clare told herself she had imagined a faint note of hurt in Diego's voice. 'It was just sex. It wasn't as if it meant anything to either of us.' She assured herself that her emotions had not been involved, and she was certain it hadn't meant anything to Diego. 'What happened after you were brought here?'

'I must have been knocked out cold and when I came round I was lying on a bed and a beautiful woman, who I've just learned is your sister, was lean-ing over me.' He grinned. 'For a couple of minutes I thought I'd died and gone to heaven.'

'I doubt you would be allowed in,' Clare mut-tered, feeling a hot surge of jealousy because Diego thought Becky was beautiful.

'Becky told me she had been kidnapped, but I didn't make the connection between the two of you because I believed your story that you were a nun going to teach at a Sunday school.' His expression hardened. 'You don't look at all like your sister.'

'Which explains why Becky is one of the most photographed models in the world and I'm an ac-countant,' she muttered.

Enzo halted outside a door and knocked. He looked nervous, and Clare's heart jumped into her throat. 'I wonder who Rigo is,' she whispered.

'His name is Rodrigo Hernandez and he heads the biggest drugs cartel in western Brazil, with smug-

gling routes across the borders into Colombia and
Peru,' Diego explained in a low voice. 'He also op-
erates a huge prostitution racket, has been linked to
several high-profile kidnappings and has a reputation for extreme violence.'

'Quiet,' Enzo growled, before he opened the door.
'Rigo will see you now.'

Clare was aware that her life and Becky's de-
pended on the outcome of her meeting with the dangerous man inside the room. She felt sick with fear
and her feet seemed to be rooted to the floor so that
she could not move. A hand grasped hers and she
jerked her eyes to Diego's.

'All right?' he asked softly. He squeezed her fingers when she nodded. 'That's my girl.'

As they walked into Rigo's office, Clare gained
an impression of walnut-panelled walls, a richly pat-
terned carpet and heavy velvet curtains that were
drawn across the windows and blocked out the day-
light. The stark white light from a lamp illuminated
the spirals of smoke that rose up from the tip of the
cigar that the man sitting behind the desk held clamped
between his lips.

Rodrigo Hernandez was dressed in a sober grey
suit and tie and looked more like a well-to-do lawyer
than a violent drugs lord who was one of the most
wanted men in South America. But his black eyes
were pitiless, Clare thought, and his cold smile sent
a shiver through her.

'Miss Marchant. I see you have brought a friend with you. Take a seat, both of you.'

'Diego agreed to drive me to Torrente, but I didn't tell him the real reason for my trip. He's not involved in any of this and you should let him go.'

'*Should* is not a word I am familiar with,' Rigo said in a pleasant voice that was somehow utterly terrifying. Clare looked into the black holes of his eyes and sat down abruptly before her legs gave way.

'I have the money you asked me to bring.' She put the briefcase on the desk and, at a nod from Rigo, one of his henchmen opened it and took out a number of prayer books. 'Oh.' She had forgotten about the books and blushed at the reminder of how she had deliberately misled Diego into believing she was a nun. She avoided looking at him. 'I meant to deliver them to the Sunday school.' She picked up the book of Keats's poems that she had put into the case for safekeeping and slid it on to her lap.

'Five hundred thousand pounds,' Rigo's assistant confirmed when he finished counting the money.

'Now you know that all the money is there, will you allow my sister to go free as…as was agreed?' Clare's voice faltered when Rigo stood up and walked around the desk. She held her breath as he touched her hair and wound a long auburn curl around his fingers.

'Such a beautiful colour,' he murmured. 'I sense, Miss Marchant, that you have a fiery temperament to match your hair. Men will pay a lot of money to bed a woman with spirit and passion. Your sister is free to leave, but I have decided that you will stay here and work for me.' He tightened his fingers on her shoulder and laughed when she could not repress a shudder. 'I may even decide to keep you for my own pleasure.'

Diego clenched his hand until his knuckles whitened. Rage burned inside him, but he knew he could not slam his fist into the slimeball Rigo's face and force him to take his hands off Clare. In order to protect her he must show no reaction. Act cool—that was what he had learned in prison. He couldn't allow Rigo to know how much he wanted to grab Clare and keep her safe. His only chance of saving her from being forced into prostitution, or forced to become Rigo's mistress, was to offer the drugs lord the thing he prized more than anything else. Money.

'It's my experience that spirited women are more trouble than they're worth,' he drawled. 'Miss Marchant will be more valuable to you if you demand a ransom for her.'

Clare shot him a sideways look. 'My father won't be able to raise enough money to pay another ransom,' she said in a fierce whisper. 'I don't think you're helping, Diego. Let me handle this.'

She looked across the desk at Rigo. 'I came to Brazil in good faith that you would allow me to pay for my sister's freedom and it is only fair that you should let us both go.'

Diego groaned silently when Rigo frowned. He wished Clare would let him deal with the situation but he could not help but admire her bravery and determination to rescue her sister. Most women would have gone to pieces by now, but not Clare. Some of his anger at the way she had lied to him about her identity faded, and he begrudgingly acknowledged that he understood why she had dressed as a nun to protect her from the ruthless men who had kidnapped her sister.

Rigo ignored Clare and spoke to Diego. 'Are you prepared to pay a ransom?'

'I am.'

Clare flashed Diego a rueful smile. 'It's kind of you to offer, but I don't suppose a gold prospector earns much money.'

'That's very funny.' Rigo laughed. 'I recognised you from the media's fascination with your personal life, Mr Cazorra. You are one of the richest men in Brazil and I would do better to demand a ransom for your release.'

Diego shrugged. 'I have no family who care about me, and I do not value my life enough to pay you a *centavo*. On the other hand, I will pay whatever you ask in return for releasing Miss Marchant. Name your price.'

The drugs lord gave him a calculating look. 'The Estrela Rosa.'

Diego did not hesitate. Any life was worth more than a lump of carbon, which was all a diamond was really. He was struck by the startling thought that he would give Rigo every precious gem he'd ever found to secure Clare's freedom. 'All right,' he said calmly, 'we have a deal.'

Clare looked between the two men with a sense that she was going mad. 'I don't understand.'

'The Estrela Rosa, the Rose Star, is the largest pink diamond ever to have been found in Brazil,' Rigo told her, 'estimated to be worth over a million dollars. It was discovered in the Old Betsy diamond mine by one of the mine's owners, Diego Cazorra.'

Not for the first time, Clare wondered if she was dreaming and would wake up in a minute. She stared at Diego's ripped jeans and the battered leather hat hiding his unkempt blond hair. Several days' growth of stubble covered his jaw and he looked tough and sexy and dangerously disreputable. 'You don't look like you own a diamond worth a million dollars.'

Amusement gleamed in his eyes. 'I'm overwhelmed by your flattery,' he said sardonically. He looked back at Rigo. 'Tell your bully boys who took my phone to return it and I'll arrange for the diamond to be flown to Torrente. We'll make the exchange on the airstrip once the girls are safely on board the plane.'

Time passed slowly when there was nothing to do but stare at a clock, Clare discovered. There were a hundred questions she wanted to ask Diego, but she hadn't had an opportunity to talk to him since they had returned to the room where they and Becky were being held prisoners.

'Have you paid the ransom? Can we leave now?' Becky had asked urgently after Enzo had escorted them back to the room and locked them in.

'We'll be allowed to leave as soon as a few things have been sorted out,' Clare had tried to reassure her sister. But she couldn't have sounded convincing because Becky had burst into tears.

'The kidnappers are going to kill us. I know they are. You shouldn't have come to Brazil and risked your life for me,' she'd sobbed hysterically. The strain of being held captive for a week was clearly getting to her.

'Of course I came for you, and we *will* be freed soon. Diego has arranged for a plane to collect us.' Clare tried to sound more confident than she felt. In truth, she did not understand what was happening. It seemed incredible that Diego owned a diamond mine and had done a deal to effectively buy her freedom from the traitorous double-crosser Rigo in exchange for a valuable pink diamond. It sounded like the plot of a thriller and she did not know who she could trust.

At least she was able to change out of the nun's habit into a pair of khaki shorts and a cotton vest top that she'd brought in her rucksack. She felt cooler in the lightweight clothes, at least until Diego stared at her bare legs with a glint in his eyes that made her blush.

She looked at him sitting in an armchair opposite her, his long legs stretched out in front of him and his hat inevitably pulled down over his eyes so that she thought he was asleep. Her mind flew back to the previous night and she pictured his naked body positioned over hers, the firelight flickering over his powerful musculature. Heat swept through her as she remembered how his rock-hard erection had stretched her when he'd first entered her. The few seconds of pain had quickly dissolved and been replaced with mind-blowing pleasure.

If they made it out of Torrente alive, would she ever see him again? Her common sense told her it was unlikely. She did not even know who he really was—a tough gold prospector who read poetry, or a wealthy diamond tycoon.

She froze when she suddenly realised he was not asleep and was watching her with a glint in his eyes that told her he knew she had been fantasising about him making love to her.

'*Deus*, Clare, I wish we were alone right now,' he said softly.

She snapped her eyes from him and glanced at Becky, who was standing tensely by the window. Perhaps as a reaction to the danger they were in, Clare could recall clearly events from the past, and she pictured her sister lying in a hospital bed, attached to numerous tubes and wires. It was a miracle that Becky had survived the aggressive form of leukaemia she'd contracted as a child, and Clare was determined her sister's life would not be cut short by a gang of despicable criminals.

Last night, a mixture of fear and exhaustion had played havoc with her emotions and led her to succumb to her desire for Diego. For a few blissful hours in his arms she had been distracted from the reason she had come to Brazil, but from now on she must focus on getting her sister to safety. 'All I wish is that the kidnappers would release us so that my sister and I can go home to our parents,' she said tautly.

Diego frowned. 'One thing I don't understand is why your family sent you to Brazil to pay the ransom money to the kidnappers. They must have realised the danger you would be in.'

'My father couldn't come because he is caring for my mother who is seriously ill, and I offered to rescue my sister. Dad must be frantic with worry about Becky.'

'I'm sure your father is worried about both of you.' Diego felt a flare of anger towards Clare's parents for the way they had allowed her to feel less loved than her sister. He hoped the Marchants realised how incredibly courageous their older daughter was.

His phone rang and he had a brief conversation in Portuguese. 'Your wish is about to be granted,' he told Clare. 'The plane that will take us to Manaus has landed at Torrente airport.'

It was not a proper airport, just a single runway at the edge of the town, surrounded by dense jungle. As the Jeep driven by Enzo pulled up next to a hangar, Clare saw a sleek private jet sitting on the runway with its engines running. She gripped Becky's hand. 'In a couple of minutes we will be on that plane and your ordeal will be over.'

Becky was white-faced and close to hysteria. 'Something is going to go wrong; I know it is.'

Clare looked at Diego. 'What are we waiting for? I thought the arrangement was for us to board the plane before you give the diamond to Rigo.'

'Rigo got here before us,' he said tensely. 'He's already on the jet. The pilot messaged me to say he's been forced to hand over the diamond.'

'Then we need to get on the jet and be ready to leave.' Clare gave a startled cry when Diego caught hold of her arm and pulled her close to him.

'I want you and Becky to get on to the plane that you can see at the far end of the runway.'

Clare stared in the direction he was pointing and frowned. 'Does it even fly? It looks like a plane from the Second World War.'

'It's a Dakota transport plane which regularly brings supplies to Torrente from Manaus. The pilot is expecting us. Tell him to be ready to take off as soon as I get on board.'

'But why can't we leave on the jet?'

Over Clare's shoulder, Diego watched Rigo walk across the runway and get into a car, leaving behind a group of armed men. *They're unlikely to be waiting to welcome the Marchant sisters on to the jet*, he thought cynically. The situation was becoming more dangerous by the minute and there was no time to explain things to Clare. He looked into her wide blue eyes and saw her fear that she was trying to hide. For reasons he couldn't explain he felt a peculiar tugging sensation in his heart. 'You have to trust me,' he said gruffly. He pushed her towards the Dakota. 'Go. Now.'

You have to trust me.

Diego's words replayed in Clare's head as she peered through the plane's window, hoping to catch sight of him in the deepening twilight. She could not think clearly above the roar of the Dakota's engines and the sound of Becky crying. *'We have to go, we have to go,'* her sister sobbed. 'Please, Clare, tell the pilot to take off before the kidnappers come for us.'

'We must wait for Diego. I'm sure he'll be here any minute.'

Where *was* he? Clare's heart leapt when she saw him by the hangar. But he wasn't alone. Shock jolted through her when she recognised that the man Diego was talking to was one of the kidnappers who had been with Enzo when she had been taken from the cave in the rainforest. In disbelief she watched Diego and the kidnapper briefly hug each other before the two men started to run towards the plane.

Becky was still crying. *'Please*, Clare, let's go now.'

Clare had a split second to make a decision. Should she tell the pilot to take off, which would ensure her

sister's safety? Or should she wait for Diego to board
the plane with one of the kidnappers? She felt sick.
Was Diego somehow involved with Rigo and his
criminal gang?

With a flash of clarity she understood that he must
have pretended to make a deal with the drugs lord to
buy her freedom. Of course he wouldn't have given
away a diamond worth a million dollars to save her.
She had been so *stupid* to have been blinded by his
handsome face and laid-back, sexy charm.

'Sit down and fasten your seat belt,' she ordered
Becky as she ran to the front of the plane and spoke
to the pilot. 'We're ready to take off, right now.'

Back on the ground, Diego had breathed easier once
he'd watched Clare and Becky board the Dakota. He
was fairly certain none of Rigo's men had seen them
climb into the transport plane. With luck he would
be able to join the girls without being seen and the
plane would take off from the airstrip before the
gang members realised that their quarry had escaped.

He'd guessed that Rigo had planned to have the
three of them killed. The time he'd spent in prison had
taught him how ruthless criminals' minds worked,
and Rigo was more ruthless than most. He hoped
the gathering dusk would hide him as he stepped out
from the doorway of the hangar, but a voice speaking in Portuguese stopped him.

'Not so fast. Put your hands in the air.'

Slowly, Diego turned around and did a double take as he recognised a face from the past. 'Miguel?'

'*Santa Mãe! Diego*, is it really you?' The other man lowered his gun. 'The last time I saw you was in prison.'

'Nearly twenty years ago.' Diego pictured two teenage boys being escorted by prison guards to an overcrowded cell, hearing the taunts from the other prisoners, terrified of what would happen to them.

'You saved my life,' Miguel said hoarsely, 'and had your ear cut off by the other prisoners as punishment for protecting me. I've never forgotten.'

Nor had Diego forgotten, despite trying to block out the memories of hell. Like him, Miguel had been on remand and awaiting trial to prove he was innocent of the crime he had been accused of. 'Why are you working for a shit like Rigo?'

Miguel shook his head. 'He threatened my family. But my parents are both dead now and I don't care if Rigo kills me for helping you to escape. I owe you, my friend.'

'Rigo isn't going to kill either of us,' Diego said grimly. 'Come with me.' He swore as he heard the roar of the Dakota's engines. 'Quickly! Our chance to escape is about to take off.'

Clare held her breath as the plane lifted off the runway. Becky was still crying, and she gripped her sister's hand. 'It's all over, Becky. You're safe and we're going home.'

But what about Diego? her conscience asked. She had rescued Becky, but what if she had been wrong to think Diego was involved with Rigo? She had seen him talking to one of the kidnappers, she reminded herself. She'd made the right choice to leave him behind, hadn't she?

'*Deus*, Clare, why didn't you wait for me?'

She gasped, wondering if she had imagined Diego's voice. But as she jumped up from her seat and looked towards the back of the plane, she saw him emerge from the cargo hold, followed by the man she'd seen him talking to on the ground who she knew was a member of Rigo's gang.

Clare's immediate instinct was to protect Becky and she stood in front of her and glared at Diego. 'Keep away from my sister. I know you work for Rigo. And this man—' she indicated the man who had boarded the plane with Diego '—is one of the kidnappers who met me at the cave.'

Diego shook his head. 'Clare, it's all right. Miguel is my friend from many years ago.' He put his hand on her arm and swore when she hit him. He saw genuine fear in her eyes and it hurt him more than it should to realise she was afraid of him.

'You crazy little wildcat,' he growled. 'I kept you safe on the journey to Torrente and spent two days up to my neck in mud. You let me believe you were a nun and made me feel guilty for wanting you. You've cost me a rare diamond worth a fortune. And, worst of all, I haven't drunk a single beer since I had the dubious pleasure of meeting you. But, even after all of that, *you still don't trust me.*'

He threw off his hat and seized her in his arms, holding her wrists behind her back so that she could not fight him as he lowered his face to hers. 'So I guess I have nothing to lose,' he muttered against her lips before he captured her mouth in a punishing kiss that demanded her total subjugation, demanded her soul—and laid claim to her heart.

Clare's common sense told her not to respond to the kiss, but she was outvoted by her body that capitulated with shameful willingness to Diego's mastery. She melted into him, seduced by the hardness of his muscles and sinews and the strength of his whipcord body pressed against hers. He was so much taller than her and, with a muttered oath, he lifted her off her feet to bring her mouth level with his and tangled his hand in her hair to prevent her from trying to escape.

But Clare was burning up in the wildfire heat of Diego's hunger. His mouth was utterly addictive and she wrapped her arms around his neck to allow him to increase the pressure of his lips sliding over hers as he deepened the kiss and coaxed her tongue into an intimate dance.

Reality faded. After everything that had happened in the past few days, Clare no longer knew what reality was. But Diego felt real and solid and nothing else seemed to matter except that he brought her senses alive and made her want to leave behind her safe, sensible life and take a leap into the unknown.

When he tore his mouth from hers and set her back on her feet she stared at him dazedly, slowly becoming aware once more of the rumble of the plane's engines and the realisation that Diego looked furious.

He pushed her down into a seat and leaned over her. 'I swear you would test the patience of a saint. If I hear another word from you for the rest of the flight I'll show you just how *unsaintly* you make me feel, *anjinho.*'

CHAPTER SEVEN

'CLARE, WAKE UP. The helicopter has come for you.'

'What…helicopter?' Struggling to surface through a haze of sleep, Clare forced her eyes open and looked groggily at her sister sitting next to her. She remembered they were on the plane, but the Dakota's engines were silent. 'When did we land? We're at Manaus Airport, I suppose.' Memories of their narrow escape from the kidnappers reminded her that her rescue mission would not be completed until her sister was safely back home. 'I doubt there are direct flights from here to London so we'll have to catch a connecting flight to Rio before we can fly to England.'

'Calm down. We're in Rio,' Becky told her. 'We flew through the night from Torrente and landed a few hours ago. It's morning now. You've slept for twelve hours, but Diego didn't want to disturb you.'

Fat chance, Clare thought sardonically. She found his brand of raw sexual magnetism deeply disturbing. 'Where is Diego, anyway?' She glanced around the empty plane.

'He had to go to his office. Before he left, he arranged for me to fly first class to London. My flight leaves soon, which is why I decided to wake you to say goodbye.'

Clare noted that her sister looked remarkably well after her kidnap ordeal. They had both shed tears of relief as the Dakota had flown away from Torrente and the realisation had sunk in that the danger was over. Becky had kept saying how brave Clare had been, but her praise had increased Clare's sense of guilt that she would never have made it to Torrente without Diego and she *should* have trusted him when he had done so much to protect her.

'Surely Diego has booked us both on to the flight to England?' She remembered his anger when she had accused him of being a member of Rigo's criminal gang. 'Or does he expect me to sit in the luggage hold?'

Becky laughed. 'You must have been in a deep sleep if you don't remember that you'll be staying in Brazil to work for the Cazorra Corporation. Diego told me you are going to run a PR campaign for an associate company he is opening in Rio under the brand name of Delgado Diamonds, which his business partner launched so successfully in Europe.'

'Just a minute...' Clare tried to make sense of her sister's words but Becky carried on talking.

'I told Dad about your plans when I phoned home to let him know we're both safe and he's excited that it will be a fantastic opportunity for A-Star PR. Running an advertising campaign for a huge international company like the Cazorra Corporation will really open doors for the A-Star agency. And it's all down to you, Clare.' Becky gave Clare a hug. 'Dad thinks you're amazing, and so do I. You saved my life and I'm so pleased you're being rewarded with the chance to further your career, as well as spend time with Diego.'

'I'm not…'

'It's all right; you don't have to tell me anything.' Becky misunderstood Clare's attempt to interrupt. 'It was clear from the way Diego kissed you last night that there's something going on between you personally as well as professionally. Just be careful. Diego Cazorra has heartbreaker stamped all over him.'

'*Becky!* Will you listen to me?' Clare's frustration bubbled over. 'There's been a misunderstanding. I'm flying back to England with you.' She searched through her rucksack and in exasperation tipped its contents on to her lap. 'I know my passport was in here.'

'Oh, I gave it to Diego so that he could arrange a permit to allow you to work in Brazil.' Becky stood up. 'It's not surprising you're feeling confused after everything that's happened. I've got to go, or I'll miss my flight. Diego's PA will be able to explain things more clearly.'

By the time Clare had stuffed her belongings back into her rucksack and hurried down the steps of the Dakota, her sister had disappeared into the airport terminal.

'Miss Marchant?' She turned towards the voice and saw an elegant-looking woman with dark hair and an exotic olive complexion. 'My name is Juliana Alvez, Mr Cazorra's personal assistant. If you would like to come with me, Diego has scheduled a meeting with you at twelve o'clock to discuss your new role.'

Clare was conscious that her shorts were creased after she had slept in them and her hair was a wild tangle of untidy curls, in contrast to Juliana's sleek chignon and sophisticated cream skirt and jacket.

How *personal* was Diego's personal assistant? she wondered, hating herself for the hot surge of jealousy that swept through her. Once again she had a sense that her life was spinning out of her control.

'That's good, because I have many questions for Diego,' she told Juliana with an air of calm composure that disguised her anger at the way she had been outmanoeuvred.

A helicopter flight over the city gave Clare spectacular views of the iconic landmarks of Rio de Janeiro, where the coastline was met by steeply sloping hills. Sugarloaf Mountain and the towering peak of Mount Corcovado with its famous statue of Christ the Redeemer dominated the skyline. The chopper swooped over beautiful Copacabana beach before it landed on the helipad at the top of a skyscraper building that looked over the bay.

'Where are we?' Clare asked Diego's PA as she followed her inside what appeared to be a luxurious

boutique hotel. The whole beach-facing side of the
building was glass so that even the corridors offered
views of the sea.

'The helipad has direct access to Diego's private
penthouse apartment,' Juliana said. 'He owns the
whole skyscraper and the Cazorra Corporation's offices are on the lower floors.' She opened a door
and ushered Clare into an enormous suite. 'This is
where you will be staying. You have a personal maid,
Vitoria, who will look after you, and I will return
just before twelve to take you to Diego.'

Clare felt decidedly out of place in her crumpled
clothes as she explored the elegant sitting room, huge
bedroom and en suite bathroom with a sunken bath
the size of a small swimming pool. The decor of
muted shades of blue and cream, and dove-grey velvet carpets, was sophisticated but impersonal. She
found it hard to imagine Diego living in the penthouse when he had admitted that he loved the wild-
ness of the rainforest.

From the bathroom she heard the sound of the
bath filling and headed towards it. The maid, Vitoria, was readying an enticing bubble bath.

'Mr Cazorra said you would like to take a bath,'
Vitoria explained as she added fragrant oil to the
water and the room became infused with the scent
of an English rose garden. The thought of sinking
into the fragrant foaming water was too irresistible for Clare to argue and, after she had bathed,
she made use of the luxurious body lotion provided

and used a hairdryer to tame her auburn curls into glossy waves.

Returning to the bedroom, she found that the maid had laid out a peacock-blue silk dress by a famous European designer. There were shoes to match the dress and exquisite underwear, all in Clare's size, but when she searched the room she could not find her rucksack containing the few items of clothing she had brought to Brazil.

The maid's excellent grasp of English suddenly seemed to desert her when she was asked about the rucksack. 'I do not know where is your bag, but you no need it, because Mr Cazorra has supplied clothes for you to wear during your visit.' Vitoria opened the wardrobe to reveal dozens of outfits, mostly in bright colours that Clare would not have had the confidence to choose for herself, preferring to stick to a safe palette of navy and taupe.

Unless she was prepared to meet Diego wearing a towel, she had no choice but to put on the dress, Clare realised. When she looked in the mirror she was forced to concede that the designer was a genius who had turned a piece of fabric into a garment that was both elegant and sexy in the way it flattered her hourglass figure. The three-inch stiletto-heeled shoes made her appear taller and slimmer, but she firmly reminded herself that she was only borrowing the clothes until she saw Diego and she would insist that her rucksack was returned to her.

He had gone to great lengths to arrange for her

to remain in Brazil rather than fly back to England with Becky. The question uppermost in her mind was why. He had been angry that she'd fooled him into believing she was a nun, and understandably furious that she had told the pilot to take off from Torrente without him.

She felt guilty about her behaviour and uncomfortable at the prospect of seeing him again, especially when she remembered them making love in the cave. Colour flooded her cheeks as she recalled her wanton response to him. The time they had spent together in the rainforest seemed like a dream and she had discarded her inhibitions along with her virginity. But now she was back to reality, back to being ordinary Clare Marchant, and she wondered what Diego wanted from her.

His PA could not hide her surprise when she saw Clare's transformed appearance. As she followed Juliana along a corridor to Diego's office, Clare was conscious of the sensual slide of the silk underwear and dress against her skin. Was it because she was no longer a virgin that her senses seemed heightened and she was intensely aware of her femininity?

Juliana opened a door and ushered her into a large modern office. Clare had a vague impression of chrome and black glass furnishings and a stunning view of the ocean, but her attention was riveted by the man standing next to the window, who was familiar and yet almost unrecognisable.

From across the room Clare saw the predatory

gleam in Diego's silver-grey eyes that reminded her of the unnerving stare of a wolf stalking its prey. But every other aspect of his appearance was different from the rough, tough gold prospector she'd met in the rainforest.

His jeans and T-shirt had been replaced with a superbly tailored charcoal-grey suit teamed with a crisp white shirt and grey tie. Although his hair was still below collar length and covered his ears, it had been tamed into a sleeker style, and the blond stubble on his jaw was now trimmed close to his skin so that he looked groomed but dangerously sexy.

He waited until his PA had closed the door and watched Clare take a deep breath and walk across the room towards him before he spoke.

'The first time I saw you at the convent I knew there was something not quite right about innocent Sister Clare. I've got it now. It's the sexy wiggle of your hips when you walk.' His voice hardened. 'I should have listened to my instincts that said you were not a nun. But you *are* a liar, like most women.'

She flushed but refused to drop her gaze. 'That's a very sweeping generalisation, and in my case it's *not* true. I am usually honest, but I was persuaded by the Mother Superior to dress like a nun because I hoped the kidnappers would be more willing to release my sister. I didn't expect a…situation to develop between us.'

Clare ignored Diego's snort of derision and sat down on the chair he indicated. She felt as if she was being interviewed when he settled himself in his executive leather chair and surveyed her across his desk.

'I have explained why I couldn't be honest about my identity, but you lied too. You let me think you were a gold prospector.'

'It wasn't a lie. I *am* a gold prospector and I search for gold deposits in the Amazon basin. When I get the opportunity, I still join a team of miners and go into the Old Betsy mine to look for diamonds. For the rest of the time I am here running the Cazorra Corporation. But I get restless after I've been in the city for too long.'

Beneath his designer suit and his veneer of wealth and sophistication was the Diego she had first met, who felt more at home in the rainforest, and who had made love to her and kept her safe in his arms throughout the night. Clare forced her mind away from the evocative memories.

'Why have you brought me here? Why did you tell my sister I will be working for you, and why have you provided me with a wardrobe of designer clothes? I don't know what game you are playing, Diego.' Frustration edged into her voice when his familiar, faintly cynical smile gave no clue to his thoughts. 'I want to go home.'

'You seem to have forgotten something.' Beneath his sardonic drawl Clare heard anger in his voice, and she felt a ripple of unease when she noted that his grey eyes were as hard as steel. 'You seem to have forgotten that I secured your release from Rigo by giving him the Estrela Rosa diamond. In effect, I bought you for one million dollars.'

'Of course I hadn't forgotten.' She bit her lip, thinking of the huge debt. 'As soon as I get home I will make it my priority to work out how I can repay you.'

'It will take you years to earn a million dollars,' he said bluntly. 'I was thinking of a more personal method by which you could repay your debt. By agreeing to be my mistress,' he elucidated when she looked at him blankly.

Clare felt a sharp pain beneath her breastbone, as if she had been stabbed through the heart. She was shocked by how hurt she felt. She *knew* that the night they had spent together in the cave had meant nothing to Diego, and she told herself it meant nothing to her. Anger came to her rescue and made her blink back the stupid tears that she would have rather died than let him see.

'Let me get this straight. You're suggesting that I could pay off my debt by having sex with you? How would that work exactly? Should I draw up a spreadsheet, and every time you have me will mean that I can tick off another few thousand dollars? How much is the going rate for sex?' Her lip curled with disgust. 'Is blackmail the only way you can get a woman? You really *must* be desperate.'

Diego's eyes narrowed. 'Careful of your sharp tongue, *querida*, and you can drop the act of outraged virgin. You gave your virginity to me while you were fooling me that you were a nun. *Deus*—' he slammed his hand down on the desk, making Clare jump '—have you any idea how guilty I felt for leading you astray from what I believed was the chaste life you had chosen?'

She flushed. 'I'm sorry that I lied to you.'

He leaned back in his chair and studied her in silence for several minutes. 'Sex with you was good, I'll grant you, but not so good that you can repay me the value of my diamond by lying on your back a few times,' he said coldly. 'I want more than your body, *anjinho*. I also want your brain—' he gave her a mocking smile '—specifically, your expertise as a PR consultant.'

Despite hating him at that moment, Clare was curious. 'What do you mean?'

'I've looked up reports about A-Star PR, and I'm impressed by the agency and by your leadership. You have run several high-profile PR campaigns for businesses in the UK and I am interested in what you might be able to provide for me. You may have heard of the jewellery company Delgado Diamonds?'

She nodded. 'The London store in Mayfair is always busy, and I believe it was recently granted a Royal warrant.'

'My business partner Cruz Delgado established the business a few years ago when he opened the first store in Paris. Cruz has a family now and wants to cut back on work commitments. He will continue to be CEO of Delgado Diamonds in Europe and I have bought the franchise to open Delgado-Cazorra Diamonds stores in the whole of South America. The first DC Diamonds shop will be launched here in Rio. But there is a problem.'

Diego ran a hand through his hair and saw Clare's eyes dart to his mutilated ear that he had unwittingly exposed. He quickly lowered his hand and his jaw hardened. 'The PR agency I originally hired to plan an advertising strategy has failed to come up with any inspirational ideas, and now the opening of the store is fast approaching but hardly anyone knows about the launch. It's partly my fault for taking my eye off the ball, but I've been distracted...' He trailed off. 'This is an opportunity for a PR expert, possibly you, to impress me by organising an aggressive marketing campaign with the aim of making every household in Brazil aware of DC Diamonds.'

'When is the flagship store due to open?'

'Three weeks from now.'

'Three *weeks*! The kind of multi-strategy campaign you want would take a few months to organise.'

He shrugged. 'If you don't think you can do it, I'm sure I will have no trouble finding a PR agency that will seize the opportunity to represent a globally successful company, which the Cazorra Corporation is.'

'I didn't say that I can't do it,' Clare said quickly. 'It will be a challenge, but it's not impossible.'

'After looking at your portfolio I am confident of your ability to promote DC Diamonds. In the expectation that you would accept the commission I ordered new clothes for you that are more suitable for your role than a pair of shorts, or a habit and veil,' he added drily.

Diego watched rosy colour flare on Clare's cheekbones and pictured her face flushed with sexual arousal when she had lain beneath him in the cave and he had nudged her thighs apart so that he could make love to her. The ache in his gut, which had started when she had walked into his office looking as sexy as sin in a dress that clung to every delectable dip and curve of her body, intensified to a sharp tug of desire.

There was no reason for her to refuse what was, in his opinion, an extremely fair offer that would allow her to repay her debt. Her hesitation fuelled his impatience to conclude their discussion so that he could do what he had wanted to do since she had walked into his office—namely, make love to her on the nearest flat surface, which happened to be his desk.

'Can I assume that you want A-Star PR to be given the commission to run an advertising campaign to promote DC Diamonds?'

'Of course I do. As you pointed out, every PR agency would seize the chance to work for the Cazorra Corporation.' Clare looked at Diego and hated the way her heart flipped as she watched his mouth curve into a sexy smile. 'But I assume that you will only give me the contract if I agree to *all* your terms and work for you in the bedroom as well as the board-room?'

'It's a fair deal.'

She stood up and drew herself to her full height, grateful that her high heels gave her a few much-needed extra inches as she struggled to hide her disappoint-ment. It would have been a huge boost to her career and to the reputation of the A-Star agency if she'd se-cured a commission with the Cazorra Corporation. Her father would have been proud of her, and she would have shown Mark Penry she couldn't care less that he'd cheated the day after he had told her he was in love with her.

With a sudden flash of insight Clare realised she did not need to prove she was worthy of her fa-ther's love. Nor did it matter that she didn't share her sister's stunning supermodel looks. The trip into the rainforest had shown her she was capable of more than she'd believed, and nothing, not even the career opportunity Diego had dangled in front of her, was worth sacrificing her self-respect for.

Head held high, she marched across the office and yanked open the door before swinging round to face him. 'You know what you can do with your job offer. I won't take either of the positions, but I *will* find a way to repay you the value of the Rose Star diamond, even if I have to scrub floors and clean toilets to earn extra money. You did not buy me, Diego, because I was not and never will be for sale.'

It was an impressive exit line, she commended

herself as she walked out and slammed the door behind her. Unfortunately, she had to spoil it moments later and go back into the room. 'You have my passport and I would like you to return it.'

Even wearing three-inch heels, Clare had to tilt her head to look at Diego's face. She had not expected him to be standing by the door when she opened it and almost collided with him. He was unsettlingly close and her senses quivered as she inhaled an evocative scent of sandalwood cologne mixed with a sensual musk of maleness that was uniquely him.

His expression was unreadable. 'You can have it back once I have confirmation that you are not pregnant.'

Diego waited for a heartbeat and watched the colour drain from Clare's face. 'You were a virgin and therefore I assume you were not prepared for sex any more than I was when we made love in the cave.'

The prospect that she might have conceived his child evoked mixed emotions in him, chiefly anger with himself that he had been so crassly irresponsible. He had never had unprotected sex before, and it was no excuse that the night he had spent with Clare in the rainforest had seemed unreal. The stark reality was that he could have fathered a child with her.

Deus, the idea that he was no better than his own father filled him with shame. But he would not abandon his baby as his father had done. His experiences had shown him that a child needed a father. He thought of Cruz's baby twin boys who were growing up with loving parents, and Diego felt a curious tug on his heart as he imagined himself holding his own son or daughter in his arms. Children were so vulnerable. He had never understood how the man whose genes he carried could have been utterly uninterested in the offspring he had carelessly fathered. One thing was certain, he could not allow Clare to return to England while there was a chance she was carrying his baby.

'I'm sure I'm not pregnant,' she said in a strained voice.

'Are you saying you are on the pill or used some other form of contraception?'

'No. But I'd only finished my period a few days before we had sex.' Clare told herself it was ridiculous to feel embarrassed discussing intimate details about herself when Diego knew her body more intimately than any other man. 'It's a biological fact that women are at their least fertile in the first few days of their monthly cycle.'

'We are not talking about women in general; we're talking about you and the fact that you could have conceived my child,' Diego said bluntly. 'When will you know?'

'In a little less than three weeks.' Her period came regularly every twenty-one days. 'There's no reason why I can't go back to England, and if…if the worst *has* happened, of course I'll phone you.'

'So you would consider being pregnant the worst thing to happen?'

Clare bit her lip. 'I…I don't know how I would feel if I was actually going to have a baby. It's not something I'd thought about at this stage of my life,' she admitted. But now she was forced to think about the full implications of possibly being pregnant—and she realised with a jolt of surprise that being a mother would not be the worst thing to happen. She enjoyed her career and felt proud that her father had put her in charge of A-Star PR. But any job seemed unimportant when she imagined holding her own baby in her arms. Her and Diego's baby, she amended as she glanced up and found him watching her. She wished she knew what he was thinking. 'What I meant was that it wouldn't be great news if I found out I was going to be a single parent.'

'That won't happen. My father abandoned my mother when she was pregnant but I will not allow history to repeat itself. If you are expecting my baby I will support you and the child. I can't allow you to leave Brazil until we know.'

'You can't force me to stay. It's preposterous.' Clare's anger was mixed with panic that Diego was powerful enough to do whatever he wanted. But, deep down, she felt strangely reassured that he had said he would support his child, unlike his own father, who had consigned Diego and his mother to a life of poverty in a *favela*. She reassured herself that statistically the likelihood of conceiving early in her monthly cycle was virtually zero.

'Three weeks is not long, and the time will pass quickly while you are working on the PR contract for DC Diamonds.'

She stared at his chiselled features as if they might give some clue to his thoughts. If he really meant to award her the contract she would be a fool not to accept it. 'I'll be happy to work on the advertising campaign, but that's all. You can't force me to be your mistress.'

His lazy smile caught her off guard. He was altogether too sexy for her own good, she thought darkly. But her traitorous body did not care that he was danger with a capital D. A swift downwards glance revealed the hard points of her nipples jutting beneath her silk dress. She instinctively stepped away from him and found herself with her back against the wall as he moved closer, his wolf's eyes gleaming as he cornered his prey.

'I have never forced a woman in my life and I don't intend to start with you, my little wildcat.' Diego's voice deepened and took on a sensual note that made Clare feel as if thick treacle was trickling over her. He placed his palms flat on the wall on either side of her head and watched the jerky rise and fall of her breasts. 'We both know you will come willingly to my bed whenever I decide to have you.'

'The hell I will.'

His outrageous arrogance fuelled her temper. As

he lowered his head and angled his mouth over hers, she stiffened, determined to deny him a response. And she might have succeeded if he had claimed her lips with demanding passion, as she expected him to do. But he did not play fair and took her breath away with a kiss that was as gentle as the brush of a butterfly's wings. He took little sips from her mouth, tasting her, tantalising her. His unexpected tenderness evoked a sensation like a knife being twisted in her stomach and desire flooded through her and pooled, hot and urgent, between her legs.

If she could not fight herself, what chance did she stand against Diego's potent sensuality? Clare thought despairingly. He was not using his superior strength to demand her response, he wasn't even touching any part of her body except for her mouth, but when he deepened the kiss she capitulated and parted her lips to allow him to slide his tongue between them. He continued to kiss her unhurriedly and with such exquisite eroticism that she moaned softly and swayed towards him, longing for him to press his body against hers.

She could have cried with disappointment when he lifted his mouth from her lips and stepped away from her. To give him credit, he did not taunt her for her pathetic weakness, and the sultry glint beneath his half-closed eyelids betrayed his hunger.

'In a moment, Juliana will take you to meet the staff who will assist you with the DC Diamonds PR campaign. If you need to leave the Cazorra building for any reason, whether work related or for personal reasons such as shopping, you will be accompanied at all times by either me or a bodyguard.'

'Is that really necessary? My sister was targeted because she is a famous model and easily recognisable, but kidnappers won't be interested in me.'

'I am not prepared to take the risk. While you are working for me, you are my responsibility.' Diego's firm tone dared her to argue. 'I have assigned Miguel to take care of you.'

'*Miguel!* You've asked one of Rigo's thugs to be my bodyguard?' Clare pictured the man who had come to the cave with the other kidnapper, Enzo. 'I'd prefer to go out alone and take my chances. I know you said Miguel is your friend from years ago, but…'

'But you still don't trust me,' Diego finished her sentence grimly. '*Deus*, without my help, you and Becky would still be trapped in Torrente and at Rigo's mercy. I have asked Miguel to protect you because he is the best person to do so. Many years ago I saved his life. In Brazil it is regarded as a lifelong debt of honour, and Miguel would willingly give his life to keep you safe because I have asked him to.'

Clare wanted to ask him more details of his friendship with Miguel, but Diego changed the subject. 'This evening I am hosting a party at my nightclub and I want you to act as my hostess.' The hard expression in his eyes challenged her to refuse, but she had decided there was no point in arguing with him when he was obviously determined to have his own way.

His brows lifted as if he was surprised by her sudden compliance. He held open his office door, but as she was about to step into the corridor he traced his thumb pad lightly across her swollen, kiss-stung lips. 'I suggest you go to the cloakroom and repair your make-up, unless you want the other members of staff to know that you have been thoroughly kissed by the boss,' he drawled.

Swallowing down a rude retort, she nevertheless deemed it wise to take his advice, and groaned when she saw in the mirror her swollen mouth and dishevelled hair. Diego was right, she looked utterly ravished. Her inability to resist him was humiliating. She *must* not allow him to kiss her again, she told herself sternly. From now on she would be a model of businesslike efficiency, and she was determined to organise a PR campaign for DC Diamonds that would impress Diego with her professionalism.

CHAPTER EIGHT

CLARE RAN HER hand down her gold-sequined dress, relieved to find that the low-cut evening gown with a side-split skirt, which she had worried was too flamboyant and revealing, was a perfect outfit to wear to Diego's nightclub and casino, Kasbah.

The club was a huge venue with numerous bars and dance floors, an enormous gambling suite equipped with poker tables, roulette wheels and slot machines, and in the centre of the club was a revolving stage lit by glittering chandeliers suspended from the marquee-like ceiling. The decor was over-the-top opulent and had been designed to represent a Sultan's harem. Rich purple carpets, gold silk wallpaper and plush velvet seating gave the interior a sensual feel that was enhanced by discreet lighting and the throb of deep bass music.

Diego had arrived at the club before Clare. His PA had explained that he wanted to watch the final rehearsal by the dancers who would be performing during the evening. Juliana had also told her that the party was a fund-raising event for the Future Bright Foundation—a charity set up by Diego and his business partner Cruz Delgado to provide education and college funds for young people living in *favelas*.

It had been left to Miguel to drive Clare to the club. The bodyguard had obviously detected that she felt wary of him and had reiterated Diego's assurance that he would protect her with his life if necessary.

'Diego said you and he were friends many years ago. Where did the two of you meet?' she'd asked, thinking that she might learn more about Diego's past.

But Miguel had given her an odd look and murmured, 'You'll have to ask Diego that question.'

Clare told herself that the mystery surrounding Diego was none of her business. In a few weeks she would go home to England and never see him again. *Unless she was pregnant with his child.* The thought slipped into her mind and she felt a flutter of nerves in her stomach. There was no point worrying about it when the chances that she had conceived were so unlikely, but she couldn't stop wondering if Diego's baby was developing inside her.

She forced her mind back to the present. The guests would be starting to arrive soon and she was wondering what her duties as Diego's hostess would entail. She caught sight of him up on the stage surrounded by a group of exotic female dancers whose costumes comprised of a few strategically placed ostrich feathers.

The girls crowded around Diego, and it wasn't hard to understand why, Clare thought ruefully. He looked amazing in a black dinner suit and white silk shirt, and his tousled, over-long hair and the shadow of blond stubble on his jaw gave him a raw sex appeal that was dangerously attractive.

Although her stiletto heels made no sound on the thick carpet, he turned his head as she approached, as if a sixth sense had alerted him to her presence.

'Clare.' There was a strange huskiness in his voice and the glitter in his silver eyes sent a frisson of sexual awareness down her spine. He did not take his gaze from her as he clapped his hands and the dancers left the stage in a flurry of feathers and a flash of lissom thighs.

'Juliana said I would find you hard at work,' Clare said drily. 'At a rough estimate, I'd guess that you have slept with at least ten of the twenty girls in the dance troupe.'

He grinned. 'But not all at the same time.' The expression in his eyes became feral as he studied her. 'I knew when I picked that dress that you would look stunning in it.'

'How did you know my size?'

'I asked your sister.' He stepped closer and murmured in her ear, 'Besides, I have an excellent memory of your body, *querida.*'

Fortunately the guests began to arrive and Diego moved to greet them, but Clare's hope that she would be able to disappear amongst the crowd was thwarted when he slipped his arm around her waist and kept her clamped to his side.

'Tonight you are my hostess,' he reminded her when she suggested he might want to circulate on his own and chat to the countless beautiful women who watched him hungrily as if they wanted to devour him.

'Why do I get the feeling that you're using me as a shield? Aren't you flattered that you could have just about any woman in the room without even having to try?'

She looked up at his handsome face, expecting to see his mouth curve into an indolent smile, but he trapped her gaze and the heat in his eyes burned her. 'There is only one woman I want but she told me she's not interested,' he said softly.

Clare was aware of the pulse at the base of her throat beating so hard she was afraid it was visible through her skin. She reminded herself that Diego was a womaniser and he was flirting with her because it was second nature to him. But sexual chemistry had sizzled between them in the steamy rainforest and it was no less potent in the semi-dark nightclub with the thudding beat of the music echoing the frantic thud of her heart. She opened her mouth to reiterate what she had told him in his office, that she would not be his mistress at any price. But instead she heard herself murmur, 'I said I wasn't for sale. I never said I wasn't interested.'

* * *

What the hell had Clare meant by that? Diego wondered as he watched her walk away from him. He was damned sure she had deliberately made an excuse that she needed to visit the bathroom, and he was tempted to go after her, lock them both in a cubicle and take her up against the wall with all the finesse of a hormone-fuelled teenager.

He raked a hand through his hair, his eyes lingering on the sway of her hips and the taut curves of her bottom beneath her twinkling sequin-covered dress. He couldn't remember when he had wanted a woman as much as he wanted her. But perhaps his inexplicable possessive feeling was because there was a possibility that she was carrying his child, he told himself.

His common sense urged him to put her out of his mind. As she had pointed out, he could take his pick from any of the single females at the party, and probably a few married ones, he thought sardonically. Money was a powerful aphrodisiac, but even before he'd become a multimillionaire women had desired him; strangely, and it was a funny thing, the less he had cared, the more they'd pursued him.

Clare was the only woman who had ever stood up to him. She had even stood up to the ruthless drugs lord, Rigo. He admired her, Diego acknowledged. Hell, he liked her as well as desired her, and he knew, because he always knew with women, that she was halfway to falling in love with him. What troubled him most was the realisation that he did not want to hurt her, which of course he would. He wasn't looking for love. The blank space in his memory of what had happened when he was seventeen hid a truth about himself that he did not want to uncover. It was safer to be a playboy who did not give a damn about anyone.

Across the room he caught the eye of one of his ex-mistresses. Belinda was an attractive blonde, wearing a minuscule dress that showed off her long legs. Like most of his exes, Diego had parted from her on good terms and her body language sent him a message that she was available. He started to walk towards Belinda but then he noticed Clare standing by the bar and scanning the room for him.

The bright lights above the bar danced over her long auburn hair, which fell in rippling waves down her back and shone like silk. *Santa Mãe*, she looked as if she had been poured into the gold dress that hugged her tiny waist and framed her full breasts. She was tying him in knots, Diego acknowledged grimly. The only way to get her out of his system was to get her into his bed.

The finest champagne and exquisite canapés were served to Diego's guests, who had paid hundreds of dollars for tickets to the party, with all the proceeds going to his charity. After the cabaret came the main fund-raising event of the evening, when donated items were auctioned. Earlier, Clare had looked at the variety of items for auction, which included fabulous jewellery, a number of valuable pieces of artwork and, most astonishing of all, a sports car. The only item she considered bidding for was a rare first edition copy of poems by English Romantic poet Lord Byron, but when she saw the starting bid price she realised it would exceed her credit card limit.

In fact, the poetry book was sold for three times the amount expected. 'You looked disappointed that the bidding for Byron's poems was so high,' Diego commented.

'Surprised, but certainly not disappointed because all the money raised at the auction goes to the Future Bright Foundation, doesn't it?'

'Every dollar,' he said with quiet pride. 'The money is put to good use. Cruz and I know from our own experiences growing up in a *favela* that education is the key to escaping poverty.'

Clare looked at him closely. 'You donated the poetry book, didn't you? And then won the bid to buy it back again.'

He shrugged. 'I do the same at every fund-raising auction. When I was a young man and borrowed books from Earl Bancroft's library, reading novels and poetry opened my mind to the realisation that there was a whole world waiting for me beyond working in a mine. I hope to give all deprived children not only a dream of a better life, but the means, by educating them, to turn their dreams into reality.'

His words touched something inside Clare. 'Do you really not have any family who care about you?' she asked softly, remembering what he had told the drugs lord Rigo. 'You told me that your father abandoned your mother before you were born and you grew up living in a *favela*. Is your mother dead too?'

He shrugged. 'I don't know. I lost contact with her when I was seventeen.'

'Have you never tried to find her?'

'No.' Diego's brusque tone warned her not to ask any more questions.

'Well, here is your book to put back on the shelf in your library,' Clare said when a waiter delivered the leather-bound book to their table.

'Actually, it's yours,' Diego murmured, sliding the book towards her. 'I bid for it on your behalf.'

She shook her head. 'I can't take on any more debt when I already owe you a million dollars for the Rose Star diamond.'

'You don't owe me for the book. It's a present.'

Diego saw Clare's look of surprise and cursed himself. Why was he behaving like a damned fool in love? He was simply wooing her a little so that she would have sex with him, he assured himself as he opened the book at a random page, which happened to be Lord Byron's famous poem, *She Walks in Beauty*.

It was a poem Diego had read many times, and his eyes were drawn to Clare's lovely face as he quoted softly, '"*She walks in beauty, like the night*

Of cloudless climes and starry skies; And all that's best of dark and bright Meet in her aspect and her eyes...'"

It was the champagne making her feel light-headed, Clare told herself, not Diego's deep voice seducing her with Byron's beautiful poetry. The two men had something in common; Byron had been notorious for his scandalous affairs and Clare had no doubt that Diego's reputation as a womaniser was well deserved.

But when he asked her to dance with him she found herself being led on to the dance floor and swept into his arms. And when their eyes met and his mouth curled into a lazy smile that stole her breath she gave up trying to resist him.

They danced the night away, and by the time the party ended and Diego helped Clare into the back of the limousine before sliding in next to her, every nerve ending in her body felt ultra-sensitive. The brush of his hand on her bare arm seemed to scorch her skin, and the feel of his hard thigh pressed up against hers made her recall how thick and hard his erection had been when he had slowly entered her.

Her awareness of him intensified as they stepped into the lift, which would take them to the top floor of the Cazorra skyscraper. The doors closed, and as the lift began its smooth ascent her eyes were drawn to him. He had unfastened his bow tie and his streaked blond hair fell across his brow, adding to his rakish charm. She wondered why he suddenly looked tense. Maybe he was irritated because she was staring at him like countless women at the party had done, she thought uncomfortably.

The lift suddenly juddered to a standstill and the lights went out.

'What the hell?' Diego said tersely. The lights flickered and came on again, but the lift did not move.

'Do you think it has broken down?'

'No, I think we're stuck between floors for fun.'

Clare frowned. 'There's no need to be sarcastic.' She studied the control panel. 'There's an emergency button. Should I press it?'

'*Deus!*' Diego exploded. 'Press the damn thing and tell the maintenance staff to get us out of here right now.'

'Diego…are you okay?' Clare stared at him. His jaw was clenched and he was oddly pale beneath his tan. When he pushed his hair out of his eyes she saw beads of sweat on his brow.

'I dislike lifts.' He caught her questioning look and muttered, 'I have an irrational fear of confined spaces.' Sweat ran down his face. He swore and wrenched off his jacket. A voice speaking in Portuguese sounded over the intercom and Diego answered with a few curt words, and Clare guessed it was lucky she did not understand.

'The concierge says he has called the engineer and the lift will be repaired as soon as possible,' he relayed to her.

She couldn't disguise her shock that he had been fearless in the rainforest, and had even wrestled with a python, but he suffered from claustrophobia. 'How did you spend years working underground in mines if you hate confined spaces?'

He shrugged. 'It was the only way I could earn a living, so I had to do it or starve. Getting into a lift cage packed with men to be taken underground was hell—it still is—but fortunately the mine shafts in the Old Betsy mine are a reasonable size to work in.' He wiped a hand over his sweat-damp face and said with an attempt at humour, 'Anyway, your heart only feels like it's going to burst out of your chest for the first few hours of a shift and, however bad you feel, you just have to get on with the job.'

The discovery that Diego had a vulnerable side to him evoked a curious tug on Clare's heart. 'Do you feel this bad every time you step into a lift? That must be difficult considering you live and work in the Cazorra skyscraper.'

'I don't usually take the lift; I use the stairs.'

'But you live on the thirtieth floor.'

'It keeps me fit,' he muttered.

'So did you only take the lift tonight because of me?'

'I couldn't expect you to climb thirty flights of stairs.'

Clare bit her lip. 'You should have told me. I feel terrible. But probably not as bad as you're feeling,' she conceded, seeing the sheen of sweat on his face. 'Is there anything I can do to help?'

'Not…unless you can come up with a distraction technique to take my mind from the thought that we are trapped in a metal box,' he said through gritted teeth.

An idea came to her, and she acted without pausing to question whether it was wise or not as she stepped closer to him and cupped his face in her hands. 'Perhaps this will distract you,' she murmured before she covered his mouth with hers and kissed him.

She felt the jolt of surprise that ran through him, but he responded instantly and opened his mouth to welcome the gentle probing of her tongue. He was content to follow her lead, and as she continued kissing him she felt the terrible tension that gripped his muscles gradually lessen.

'Is it working?' She finally had to stop and allow them both to breathe.

'I'm not sure,' he said thickly. 'You'd better try again.'

He did not look quite so pale, she thought as she stood on tiptoe so that she could reach his mouth. This time he took control and deepened the kiss until Clare's senses were swamped by the taste of him, the scent of his aftershave, the feel of his strong arms sliding around her waist to pull her even closer to him—so close that she could not mistake the hard ridge of his arousal.

'Something's definitely working,' he drawled, sounding more like the laid-back Diego she knew— and did *not* love. Of course not. It was just a silly saying that had slipped into her mind.

The lift suddenly lurched and then continued its ascent. Clare sprang away from him, hot-faced with embarrassment that in trying to distract him from his phobia she had aroused him, and herself, she acknowledged ruefully as she glanced down at the outline of her nipples jutting beneath her dress.

Moments later the doors opened directly into the penthouse and she heard Diego exhale heavily as he followed her out of the lift. As they walked in silence along the hallway leading to their respective bedrooms she did not know what to think, or what was going to happen next. But she knew with sudden clarity what she wanted to happen. Becky had warned her that Diego was a heartbreaker, but Clare had no intention of letting him anywhere near her heart.

Disappointment swooped in her stomach when he walked straight past the door to his suite without trying to persuade her to sleep with him. Maybe he did not desire her as much as she'd thought.

Her room was next to his. He halted outside the door and casually swung the jacket that he was carrying over his shoulder. But there was nothing casual about the smouldering intensity in his eyes, and his voice was a rough growl that grazed her skin and sent a quiver of excitement down her spine. 'Are you going to invite me in?'

'Yes.' Simple, direct. She was tired of playing games. 'But there is a condition.'

His brows rose in silent query.

'I won't pay off my debt with sex and after tonight I will still owe you a million dollars. I'm inviting you into my bed because I want you. But I won't be your mistress. You will be my...' she had been going to say *lover*, but reminded herself that love was not involved '...stud.'

He gave a husky laugh that evoked a coiling sensation low in her pelvis. 'You are something else, Clare.' There was a curious note that she almost thought was admiration in his voice. He opened her bedroom door, placed his hand at the small of her back and pushed her into the room. 'Be careful what you wish for, *querida*.' He slid his hand down and caressed her bottom, his touch burning her through her dress. 'You want a stud and, as you can feel—' he pressed up against her so that his erection nudged the cleft between her buttocks and their clothes were a frustrating barrier '—I am very willing to oblige.'

Diego knew he was going to have to cool things down. He was fiercely tempted to drag Clare's dress up to her waist, pull her knickers down and bend her over the end of the bed so that he could take her hard and fast, the way his body was aching to do. Adrenaline was still pumping through his veins from when they had been trapped in the lift, but his urgent need to make love to her was more than a primal urge to have sex.

Deus, she had been so sweet when she had kissed him to distract him from his stupid, irrational fear. If she knew the truth of why he hated confined spaces, maybe she would understand that his gut-churning terror of being confined was not irrational. But he had never told any of his mistresses that he had been to prison, so why would he tell Clare?

He realised she was watching him with a faint uncertainty in her eyes that made him dismiss his thoughts and focus all his attention on her. She'd said she wanted a stud, but her only experience of sex was when he had taken her virginity. What she needed from him was patience and tenderness. It occurred to him that he would enjoy teaching her the many and varied pathways of pleasure that she had never experienced with any other man. Diego frowned. This possessive feeling was a new experience for him and not one that he wanted to think about too deeply.

He threaded his fingers into her hair that felt like silk against his skin and lowered his head to claim her lips in a kiss that started out as gentle. But her eager response stoked the fire inside him so that he thrust his tongue into her mouth in an erotic imitation of thrusting his throbbing arousal into her.

She tugged open his shirt buttons and ran her hands feverishly over his bare chest. He gave a half-laugh, half-groan. 'How can I make love to you slowly and gently when you are so damned hot?'

Clare curled her arms around his neck and pulled his mouth down to hers, pressing her curvaceous body up against him so that Diego could feel the hard points of her nipples scrape across his chest. 'I don't want slow and gentle. I don't mind if you are rough,' she whispered against his lips. 'I just want you now, *now*.'

'*Deus*, you will be the death of me, *anjinho*.' He ran her zip down her spine and tugged the gold dress. She wasn't wearing a bra and her bare breasts spilled into his hands, firm and plump like ripe peaches, and utterly delectable when he kissed the creamy mounds, before he closed his lips around one pouting nipple and then the other.

Her soft moans of delight nearly drove him over the edge, and when she fumbled with the zip on his trousers and her fingers brushed across his arousal he knew he had to take control. He swiftly dragged her dress over her hips so that it slid to the floor, leaving her in just a tiny gold thong and high-heeled strappy gold sandals. Diego knelt and removed her shoes and then scooped her up and deposited her on the bed, but he resisted her attempt to pull him down on top of her.

He stood at the end of the bed and pushed her thighs apart. 'I'll explain how this is going to work, *querida*. I am going to kiss every inch of your body, and I mean *everywhere*,' he warned her softly. 'Now lie back.'

* * *

He could not actually mean everywhere, Clare thought as she stretched out on top of the satin bedspread while Diego knelt above her and lowered his head to capture her mouth in a sensual kiss that added fuel to the flame of her desire. He trailed his lips over her throat and breasts, paying special attention to her nipples until she whimpered with pleasure. 'Enough,' she pleaded in a breathy voice she hardly recognised as her own.

'I've barely begun,' he told her as he moved down her body, kissing her stomach and the tops of her thighs. She trembled and instinctively tried to scissor her legs together, but he firmly held them open so that she was utterly exposed to him apart from a fragile strip of gold silk. He pushed her thong aside, and as Clare felt his silky hair brush against her inner thighs she suddenly realised that he really did intend to kiss *every* bit of her.

'I'm not sure…' It seemed like a step too far, too intimate. Yet she was curious, and her body was burning up with need that intensified when she felt his tongue flick across the tight nub of her clitoris. She jerked her hips involuntarily towards his mouth and gasped as he proceeded to lick his way inside her.

Sweet heaven… She clutched the bedspread and held on for dear life as the pressure inside her built with every thrust of his tongue, taking her higher, taking her towards ecstasy. She came so hard that it almost hurt, her vaginal muscles squeezing and contracting with fierce, fast spasms that left her wanting more.

'Please…' Was that really her voice sounding so guttural, so desperate? Clare was shocked by the intensity of her desire. Diego had called her a wildcat, and he turned her into one. With him she became wild and wanton and she practically purred with anticipation as she watched him strip and slide a protective sheath over his awesome erection.

When he dipped his head between her legs again, she made a husky protest. 'No more. I want…' Her voice faded as Diego ripped her thong apart with his teeth.

'I know what you want,' he growled as he lifted himself over her. 'You want this…'

He had tried to be gentle, Diego assured himself, but the combination of his urgency and Clare's eagerness created a simmering chemistry that was about to combust. He looked down at her gorgeous, curvaceous body, her pale thighs spread wide in readiness for him to possess her. Anticipation sharpened his desire to a primitive need he could no longer deny and he thrust into her and drove deep, drawing a gasp of surprise from her as her internal muscles were forced to stretch to accommodate his solid length.

She was so tight, so hot. He paused to give them both time to snatch a breath and felt a curious tightness in his chest when she smiled. *Deus*, she was so beautiful. The sweetness of her smile felt like a punch in his gut. What the hell was happening to him? Diego asked himself grimly. First he had quoted romantic poetry to her, and now he felt emotions surge though him that he did not dare examine.

It was just sex, he reminded himself. He was good at sex, as his numerous ex-mistresses could verify. Clare had told him she wanted a stud and he was confident he wouldn't disappoint her.

He began to move inside her, to thrust and withdraw in a powerful rhythm as he took her stroke by measured stroke while she moaned and writhed beneath him. He could feel his climax building, but he did not falter, driving into her faster, harder until she gave a keening cry and her body shuddered with the intensity of her orgasm.

It was his signal that finally he could take his own pleasure and he surged forwards once more and let himself come. The intensity of his release tore a groan from deep inside him, and in the aftermath, as his heartbeat slowed, he was strangely reluctant to move and disjoin from her.

At last he rolled away and stared up at the ceiling, searching his mind for something banal to say that would shatter the emotionally charged atmosphere. He frowned when Clare snuggled up to him. He did not do snuggling and, however good it felt to have her soft body pressed up against him, her hand resting lightly on his chest, he could not risk falling asleep in her bed. He never knew when his sleep would be disturbed by a nightmare, or what secrets his dreams might reveal.

Her long auburn eyelashes lay on her cheeks and the sound of her even breaths told him she had fallen asleep. He resisted the temptation to wake her and take her again. She would be staying in Brazil for three weeks to work on the PR campaign and that was more than enough time for him to sate his desire for her. No doubt by the time of the DC Diamonds launch he would have grown bored of her. He refused to think of the problems that would lie ahead if she had actually conceived his child.

Taking care not to disturb her, he slid off the bed and draped the bedspread over her before he silently left the room.

Clare watched Diego exit her bedroom with a sense of disbelief that was rapidly turning to anger. She had been drifting off to sleep when she'd felt him move, and at first she had thought he was visiting the bathroom. But as she watched him walk over to the door she realised that he did not intend to spend the night with her.

He'd had what he wanted, she thought bitterly. She had provided him with sex, and presumably he saw no reason to stay in her bed. Why was she surprised? She knew he was a womaniser, but she had conveniently forgotten that fact when he had deliberately seduced her with romantic poetry. She understood now that his motive for giving her the book of Byron's poems had been entirely cynical. But, like an idiot, she had been beguiled by the tender expression in his eyes and, to compound her foolishness, she had been taken in by his apparent panic attack in the lift and his confession that he suffered from an irrational fear of confined spaces. Although when she remembered his clenched jaw and how his skin had turned sickly green, she conceded that he probably hadn't been faking his claustrophobia.

She lay there for a few more minutes, but sleep was now impossible when she felt so churned up inside. Muttering an oath, she swung her feet on to the floor and pulled on Diego's shirt that he'd discarded before he'd taken her to bed.

His room was bigger than hers, she discovered when she padded down the hall and opened his door. Unlike the neutral decor of the other rooms in the penthouse, the walls of Diego's bedroom were covered in prints of the Amazon rainforest. But Clare's attention was focused on the enormous bed where he was sprawled, his broad shoulders propped against a pile of pillows. He was reading, but looked up from his book and frowned when he saw her.

'I'm surprised you didn't leave a handful of dollars on my bedside table in payment for my services,' she said tautly. 'But then I remembered that you believe I should pay off my debt to you with sex. Let's see. There's three weeks until the DC Diamonds launch. That's twenty-one nights, divided into one million dollars, which means it just cost you approximately fifty thousand dollars to have sex with me.'

To her annoyance she could not prevent her voice from trembling. 'I hope I was worth it.'

'Clare...' Diego swore beneath his breath when he noticed the glimmer of tears in her eyes. He hated that she was clearly hurt, and he was responsible. *'Querida...'*

'Don't *querida* me,' she said fiercely. 'I'm not your darling. I'm your whore. You made it perfectly obvious when you left my bed that all you want from me is sex.' She tried to swallow her tears and choked. 'You made me feel cheap.'

'Deus,' Diego growled as he leapt out of bed and strode over to her. 'That was not my intention. I thought you had fallen asleep, and I didn't want to disturb you.' He caught hold of her arm to prevent her from rushing out of the door. 'I don't sleep well, and I usually read for several hours during the night.'

'What are you doing?' Clare had tried not to stare at Diego's naked body when he'd got out of bed, but she couldn't ignore his erection that was jabbing into her thigh. She tried to move away from him, but he swept her up into his arms and held her tight against his big chest. 'I can walk back to my room,' she muttered as he carried her into her bedroom and placed her on the bed. 'Leave me alone.' She tried to turn her head away as he slanted his mouth over hers, but he cradled her cheek in his hand and smothered her protest with a sensual, evocative kiss that tugged on her treacherous heart.

'I think I've made it fairly obvious that I can't

leave you alone,' he said drily, but his sardonic tone
was laced with something deeper and more urgent.
He deftly removed his shirt from her, and his eyes
gleamed with feral intent as he ran his hands over her
body, caressing her breasts before he moved lower
and found that she was wet for him. 'I don't want to
hurt you,' he whispered against her mouth as he positioned himself over her.

But he would, she thought with a sudden fearful
insight. It wasn't his fault. He had been honest and
admitted he only wanted to have a sexual relationship with her. It was her foolish heart that was to
blame. If she had any sense she would insulate her
emotions against his impossible to resist charisma.

CHAPTER NINE

'CLARE. *DEUS,* YOU sleep like the dead!'

The sound of Diego's impatient voice forced Clare to open her eyes, and she stared at him looming over her. As always, the sight of his handsome face and his blond hair falling across his brow made her heart flip. She noted that he looked wide awake and disgustingly energetic, which was impressive as he had not left her bed until some time around two o'clock. She could not be sure of exactly when, because he always waited until she had fallen asleep before leaving her and returning to his own room.

She had accepted his reason that he never spent the entire night with her because he was a restless sleeper and did not want to disturb her, but she didn't know what caused his insomnia. There were a lot of things she did not know about him, she thought ruefully. Diego was as much of an enigma now as he had been when she had started working on the PR campaign for DC Diamonds three weeks ago.

Their schedule every day had been hectic. She

had organised a huge publicity campaign to promote
Diego's new business venture, and he had insisted
on her accompanying him in his private helicopter
to TV and radio stations in cities all across Brazil so
that he could give interviews and advertise his new
jewellery shop franchise.

She stretched her arms above her head, unaware
that the sheet slipped down to reveal her bare breasts,
or of the feral gleam that flared in Diego's eyes as
he viewed the plump mounds of flesh, each adorned
with a dusky pink nipple. 'What time is it?'

'Eight o'clock.'

'Why have you woken me up? You might be able
to function on six hours' sleep,' she muttered, 'but I
need a full eight hours.'

He gave a husky laugh that stirred Clare's body
to instant arousal. 'You need to get up, *anjinho*, because if you don't I will join you in bed, and either
way you won't get any more sleep.'

She pretended to consider. 'What will you do to
me if I refuse to get up?'

'Don't tempt me.' Beneath his playful tone was a
rougher note of raw sexual need. 'Seriously, *querida*,
I want to take you out for the day. Cruz and his wife,
Sabrina, have arrived from their home in Portugal
with their baby twins. They are renting a beachfront
villa along the coast and have invited us to spend the
day with them.'

Clare sat up and pulled the sheet over her breasts
to hide them from Diego's heated gaze. 'But tonight

is the launch party for DC Diamonds and I need to be here to oversee final preparations and deal with any problems.'

'There won't be any problems. I've seen the size of your folder of notes regarding arrangements for the party and I'm certain you have everything under control. I have been impressed with the PR campaign you organised over the past three weeks. You should be proud of yourself.'

She shot him a glance and realised he wasn't teasing her. His praise made her feel stupidly happy, but she shoved the thought to the back of her mind, along with the other thought that after tonight there would be no reason for her to remain in Brazil. Unless she was pregnant. Her heart lurched. She was only two days late, she quickly reminded herself, and in fact she felt slightly nauseous, which was usually a sign that her period was about to start.

'It will be good for you to spend the day relaxing before the party,' Diego said persuasively.

'What time are we expected to meet Cruz and Sabrina?'

'I told them we would be over in an hour.'

'Mmm...' She let the sheet slide down her body and slipped her hands under his T-shirt, running her fingertips over the golden hairs that grew thickly on his chest. 'So I can stay in bed for a bit longer. Care to join me?'

'Minx,' he growled, helping her pull his shirt over his head. Clare caught her breath when he cupped her

breasts in his palms and flicked his thumbs across
her nipples, making them tighten and tingle. Their
passion for one another had not lessened in three
weeks; in fact it seemed to intensify every time they
had sex—and they had sex a lot.

She felt hot all over as she remembered the previous day when Diego had called her into his office
to supposedly discuss the PR campaign. She should
have guessed his intention when he'd instructed his
secretary not to disturb them and locked the door. 'I
thought we were meant to be having a meeting,' Clare
had reminded him when he'd unbuttoned her blouse.

'We are. My body is going to meet with yours,
and I promise you the outcome will be very produc-
tive,' he'd told her, and had proceeded to make love
to her bent over his desk.

It wasn't just the sex that was amazing. They spent
all day every day in each other's company, either
working on the campaign or relaxing over dinner at
the penthouse or a restaurant, and they made love several times every night. The only downside was that
he never stayed all night with her. But perhaps it was
a good thing because she knew she was increasingly
in danger of falling in love with him. Waking up in
an empty bed each morning was a stark reminder
that the closeness she felt to Diego was an illusion
she would be foolish to believe might become real.

They were only half an hour late to meet their hosts,
after Diego had made love to her and then carried

her into the shower, where he had been very inventive with a bar of soap.

If Cruz and Sabrina noticed the hectic flush on Clare's face, or Diego's smug smile, they were too polite to say so. Clare liked the couple instantly. Cruz's dark, brooding good looks contrasted with his wife's English rose complexion. Lady Sabrina Bancroft, as she had been before her marriage, was elegant and refined, but she exuded a warmth and friendliness that drew people to her, which was one of the reasons, Clare suspected, that her husband was utterly besotted with her.

The couple's nine-month-old twin boys, Vitor and Henrique—named, Sabrina explained, after their two grandfathers—were adorable. Both babies had dark brown curls and green eyes, and were already displaying signs that they had inherited their father's determined personality.

Watching the little boys crawling across the rug, Clare felt an unexpected tug of maternal longing. She had never given much thought to babies, and had assumed she would have children some time in the future. But for the last few days as she'd waited anxiously for a sign that she had not conceived Diego's child, she'd found herself imagining holding her own baby in her arms.

The two men spent the morning riding jet skis on the sea, while Clare stayed on the beach and helped Sabrina chase after the babies, who were intent on crawling away from the shade of a parasol.

'Which of your godsons do you want to hold?' Cruz asked Diego after they had returned to the house.

'I don't want to show favouritism so you'd better hand me both of them,' Diego replied easily. Watching him with the baby boys, Clare felt another tug on her insides as she pictured him cradling a blond baby who was their son or daughter. *Stop it*, she told herself firmly. She *couldn't* be pregnant. The strange light-headed sensation that had swept over her before lunch, when she'd thought she might faint, had been a sign that she was stressed about tonight's party.

The buffet lunch was a relaxed meal that continued into the afternoon. While the twins napped in their prams there was a chance for the adults to chat.

'How is Earl Bancroft?' Diego asked Sabrina.

She smiled. 'Dad is very well. My father lives in a stately home in England,' she explained to Clare. 'He has opened Eversleigh Hall to the public and he seems to enjoy giving tours of the house.'

Clare suddenly made the connection. She turned to Diego. 'So the English earl who owned a diamond mine that you once worked in is Sabrina's father?'

He nodded. 'Some years after Henry sold the Old Betsy mine, Cruz and I were in a position to buy it. Cruz had earned a fortune as a banker, and I inherited money from my father's family. We decided to gamble and invest in the diamond mine, and luckily the gamble paid off.'

She was puzzled. 'I thought you didn't have any contact with your father.'

'It's true I never met him. He knew my mother had given birth to his child but he wasn't interested in finding me. He died young, but before he passed away he told his father that he had an illegitimate child in Brazil. It was a total shock when Father Vincenzi found me and gave me the news that I was my grandfather's only heir.'

'Who is Father Vincenzi?'

'He is a priest who helped me when I...' He broke off abruptly and Clare knew she had not imagined the sudden awkward silence that fell over the table, or the swift glance that passed between Cruz and Sabrina. 'The holy Father helped me when I was a young man.' Diego did not elaborate on his statement. Instead he stood up and spoke curtly to Clare. 'It's time we were leaving. I expect you'll want plenty of time to get ready for the party.'

Diego had demanded something spectacular for the launch party of DC Diamonds and, with an unlimited budget to spend, Clare had chartered one of the world's largest and most luxurious super-yachts, *Serendipity*, for the party venue.

From the balcony of her stateroom she watched helicopters flying to and fro, bringing guests out to the yacht, which was moored in Copacabana bay. She and Diego had arrived by chopper in the late afternoon, and she had spent a couple of hours checking final details with the team of chefs who were preparing canapés, and the bar staff who had created a

special cocktail in honour of DC Diamonds, which
they had named 'Bling.'

During the party, champagne fountains would
flow with Cristal, which guests could enjoy while
they watched a catwalk show. Clare had hired top
models to wear jewellery from the DC Diamonds collection. Later in the evening there would be a disco
with music provided by a world-famous DJ, and the
climax of the night was to be a firework extravaganza
viewed from *Serendipity*'s decks.

A glance at her watch revealed that the party was
due to start in fifteen minutes. All she could do now
was hope that everything went to plan. She felt a flutter of nerves in her stomach that grew stronger when
there was a knock on her door and Diego strolled in.

He had been uncommunicative when they'd left
Cruz and Sabrina, and Clare had not seen him since
they had boarded the yacht. But now her breath
caught in her throat at the sight of him in a black
tuxedo teamed with a black shirt. With his blond hair
falling over his collar and his chiselled jaw shaded
with blond stubble, he looked dangerously disreputable and utterly gorgeous.

The lazy curl of his smile told her that he had got
over his earlier bad mood, and she warned herself to
be on her guard against his sinfully sexy charm. But
the expression in his eyes was harder to decipher as
he said in an oddly rough voice, 'I have never seen
you look as beautiful as you do tonight.'

Clare spun round to the mirror to hide the fact

that she suddenly felt ridiculously self-conscious. 'It's a beautiful dress. I have to say, you have very good taste in dressing women,' she said, needing to remind herself that he probably had plenty of experience in choosing clothes for his mistresses and had not made a special effort when he'd picked a dress for her to wear to the party.

The sapphire-blue velvet gown with off-the-shoulder straps was a fishtail style, tight-fitting over her bust and hips to show off her curvaceous figure, and the lower part of the skirt flared out into a small train at the back. She had piled her hair into a loose knot on top of her head with a few tendrils framing her face. A coat of mascara on her eyelashes and a slick of pink lipgloss completed her look. She certainly did not need to wear blusher, she thought ruefully when she saw the flush on her cheeks as Diego came to stand behind her.

'You look beautiful whatever you are wearing, but my personal preference is for you to wear nothing at all,' he murmured, bending his head to feather kisses along her collarbone.

'Mmm, not very practical for the party...' She managed to keep her tone light to hide the fierce sexual excitement that made her breasts tingle.

Diego gave a sigh that sounded more like a wolfish growl. 'I can't wait until the party is over and I can have you to myself. Shall I tell you what I plan to do to you when we are alone, *anjinho*?'

'You had better not!' She laughed breathlessly and stepped away from him. It was hard to resist his charisma and sexual teasing. 'You need to go down to the main deck to greet the guests.'

He slid his arm around her waist and led her towards the door. 'I suppose so,' he said regretfully, 'but I insist that my favourite PR expert stays by my side all evening.'

Clare told herself not to read too much into Diego's words, or his attentiveness during the party. True to his word, he kept her close to him as they strolled around the yacht's ballroom and chatted with the guests. Clare sampled a couple of delicious canapés but opted for sparkling water rather than champagne, explaining that she was on duty and wanted to keep a clear head.

There was a buzz of excitement as the jewellery show was about to begin and guests took their seats on either side of the catwalk. She and Diego had front row seats with a perfect view of the models as they sauntered down the runway. The female models wore identical black full length gowns and the men were dressed in black suits so that the audience focused on the fabulous diamond necklaces, earrings and watches being showcased by the models. But Clare's attention was caught by one model in particular. *'Mark?'*

'I get the feeling you wouldn't pay me any attention even if I was butt naked.'

Diego registered the sarcasm in the female voice

and he flicked an impatient glance at the woman standing next to him. He had a vague idea that Tiffany Delany was the daughter of a diplomat, and an even vaguer memory that he might have slept with her once. She was attractive and blonde—which were his only requirements, he thought self-derisively. At least, they used to be. He looked back to the dance floor, where Clare was dancing with one of the male models. Diego's eyes roamed over her petite figure in the blue dress that hugged her curves and her auburn hair, gleaming like burnished gold beneath the disco lights, and he acknowledged that she was the only woman he wanted.

'Who'd have guessed that Diego Cazorra would suffer from woman trouble?' Tiffany drawled. 'Your little redhead must be something special—you haven't stopped staring at her. Someone ought to warn the guy dancing with her that you look like you want to kill him.'

'Don't be ridiculous.' As he strode away from the blonde he knew he should apologise for his curtness, but Tiffany had touched a nerve. Watching Clare dance with her supposedly ex-boyfriend had stirred a violent jealous rage inside Diego. *But was it a murderous rage?* He was seriously tempted to rearrange Mark Penry's pretty-boy features, but what if he had actually punched the model and seriously injured him, or worse? Was that what he had done when he was seventeen and tried to protect his mother from the man who'd been beating her? Had he punched the man with such force that he'd killed him, which was what his mother had told the police?

Although *Serendipity* was a huge yacht, it was packed with party guests and Diego felt a tightness in his chest as he pushed his way through the crowd. Memories of an overcrowded prison cell flashed into his mind. Violent, desperate men, the stench of sweat in the hot, airless cell. *He couldn't breathe.*

He ran up the stairs to the top deck, burst into his stateroom and opened the sliding glass door so that he could step on to a private deck area that was only accessible from his suite and Clare's room next door. Fresh sea air filled his lungs as he leaned against the balcony railing and fought to control the panic attack. *Deus*, was he capable of murder? Tonight had exposed the blackness in his soul.

Clare had disappeared immediately after the jewellery show and Diego had scoured the yacht for her before he'd seen her dancing with a handsome model—Mark Penry, he had learned from one of the guests. He'd instantly recognised the name as the guy who Clare had said had broken her heart. The way she had snuggled up to Penry suggested that she was still keen on her ex, and Diego had come close to striding across the dance floor and snatching her into his arms.

This was why he had never become emotionally involved with any of his mistresses. He could not risk feeling strong emotions like love or hate, jealousy or anger. Especially anger. He was afraid of what he might do if he was pushed too far. The blinding rage that had swept through him when he'd seen Clare with Mark Penry had shocked him. She meant nothing to him, he reminded himself. Sure, she was fun to be with, and the sex was good. The sex was amazing. But it meant *nothing*.

He stiffened at the sound of footsteps crossing the deck. A delicate fragrance of roses assailed his senses and Clare's soft voice made his gut twist.

'I was looking for you. The fireworks are about to start.' She came to stand beside him and Diego was bitterly aware of the immediate effect she had on his body as he felt himself harden. 'Mind you, we probably have the best view from here.'

'That's the reason I came up here,' he lied. 'You looked as though you were having fun dancing. I didn't know you had hired your ex-boyfriend for the catwalk show.' Diego despised himself for sounding like he cared, but Clare didn't appear to notice his strained tone.

'I didn't. I was shocked when I saw Mark, but he explained that he replaced Tom Vaughn, another model from A-Star PR, who should have been on the assignment but broke his ankle a few days ago.'

Some of Diego's tension eased. At least Clare had not arranged for Penry to come to Brazil. 'So, are you tempted to get back with a guy who models underwear for a living?' he said lazily.

She laughed. 'No. I realised during the one dance I had with him that he is completely self-obsessed.

He spent most of the time discussing his hair. To be honest, I don't know why I got so upset over him. I think I was flattered that he showed an interest in me.' She hesitated. 'But now that the DC Diamonds campaign is finished I have decided to fly back to England with the models. It will be company for me during the flight and give me an opportunity to catch up on what has been happening at A-Star PR while I've been away.'

Diego felt his gut give another twist. 'Do you know for certain that you are not pregnant?'

'I'm ninety-nine per cent sure. My breasts feel really sensitive, which is usually a sign my monthly period is about to start. I expect I'll be able to confirm the news you are hoping for tomorrow.'

Of course he hoped she hadn't conceived his child, Diego thought, but oddly he did not feel like jumping for joy. It was good that Clare would be going home, he assured himself. He hadn't grown bored of her yet, as he'd assumed he would, but he was confident he would have no trouble finding another woman to replace her. Meanwhile, he still had tonight with Clare. Overhead a firework exploded in a starburst of silver and gold that lit up the night sky, but he was more concerned about the imminent explosion he could feel building inside him.

'Your breasts are always sensitive,' he murmured as he pulled her unresisting body towards him and reached behind her to run her zip down her spine. Her dress fell forwards, spilling her ripe breasts into

his hands. Her nipples were already taut and he heard
her breath catch when he rubbed his thumbs over
them before he lowered his head and captured one
reddened peak between his lips.

He loved how she was so responsive. Her little
moans of pleasure drove him crazy, and with a groan
he swept her up in his arms and carried her into her
bedroom.

'Are you going to tell me now what you plan to
do with me?' she asked innocently.

Diego dropped her on to the bed and stripped with
more haste than grace. He gave a rough laugh when
her eyes widened as she watched him slide a sheath
over his massive erection. 'I think a personal dem-
onstration is necessary, *querida*.'

Clare heard a voice shouting in her dream. The shouts
grew louder and more urgent, forcing her to wake
up, and she realised that she hadn't been dreaming.
Diego was lying beside her in her bed. Light filtering
through the blinds made her realise it was morning.
He must have spent all night with her, or what had
been left of the night after they had made love numerous times until she had slumped back on the pillows, unable to keep her eyes open a moment longer.

'Diego…' She tentatively shook his shoulder but,
wherever hellish place his mind was, he was in too
deep for her to reach him. He groaned as if he was in
pain and it hurt her to see him so tormented. 'Diego,
wake up.'

His eyes opened and he sat bolt upright, his chest heaving with the force of his harsh breaths. He stared at her as if he did not recognise her.

'It's all right,' she told him softly. 'You're dreaming, that's all.'

'Clare.' He swallowed and raked his hair back, revealing his disfigured ear for a few seconds before he remembered and shook his hair forwards again.

'What was your nightmare about?'

He shrugged. 'I don't know. Nothing much.' His tone was dismissive but Clare heard a rawness in his voice that she sensed he was desperate to hide.

'It didn't sound like *nothing much.* Why won't you talk about it?' She could not contain her frustration. 'Why do you have so many secrets? Why won't Miguel tell me where the two of you met? Who cut off the top of your ear? *Why do you always shut me out?*'

The silence following her outburst simmered with tension as Diego's shocked expression turned to anger. Clare swallowed, trying to fight the feeling that she was going to be sick. But the sensation of nausea grew worse and, with a gasp, she leapt out of bed, grabbed her robe and ran into the bathroom. She did not have time to lock the door.

Oh, God, could anything be more undignified? she thought when she had finished vomiting and sat down weakly on a chair. The one and only time Diego had spent the night with her would be unforgettable for all the wrong reasons.

'Go away, please,' she muttered when he followed her into the bathroom. He ignored her and sponged her face with a damp flannel.

'Feeling better?'

She nodded, hoping he would leave. She was sure he would not answer any of her questions, and she felt emotionally as well as physically drained.

Diego hunkered down in front of her and put his hands on the arms of the chair, effectively imprisoning her. 'Good, because I've got some questions for you. Why did you buy a pregnancy test if you are so sure you're not pregnant? And for how long have you been suffering from morning sickness?'

'It's not morning sickness.' She bit her lip. 'I get seasick.'

He gave her a sardonic look. 'The yacht is anchored and the sea is as flat as a pond. Have you been sick before this morning?'

'No. But I've felt nauseous the last few mornings,' Clare admitted. 'I've been telling myself it was because my period is about to start. I bought the test just…just to be sure.' She looked down at the pregnancy test that Diego had picked up from the vanity unit and dropped into her lap.

'Let's be sure then,' he said grimly.

CHAPTER TEN

SHE COULDN'T BE PREGNANT. *But she was.* Clare stared at the two lines on the test kit and reread the instruction leaflet. Two lines indicated a positive result. Maybe the test was wrong? She knew she was clutching at straws and gripped the edge of the vanity unit as her legs almost gave way.

Diego rapped on the door, which she had locked before she had performed the test. 'Well?'

She did not answer, needing a few more minutes on her own to absorb the implications of the result. *A baby. She was pregnant with Diego's baby.* Clare studied her reflection in the mirror, surprised that she still looked the same, apart from her pallor following the bout of sickness. Of course there would not be any visible signs yet of the miracle taking place inside her body. She put her hand on her flat stomach and tried to imagine her belly swollen with her growing child.

Her emotions see-sawed between panic and an unexpected sense of elation and excitement. In a few months from now she would hold her child in her arms, and she felt a fierce sense of maternal protectiveness and determination that her child would never doubt that he or she was loved by its parents, as she had done when she was growing up and her parents had paid more attention to her sister. But how would Diego react to the news that he was going to be a father? Three weeks ago he had said he would support her if she was pregnant, but even if he was prepared to offer financial assistance she could not make him love his child, Clare acknowledged.

'Clare, are you all right?'

She could not put off opening the door any longer. Diego looked tense, no sign of his usual nonchalance on his chiselled features. 'Well?' he demanded again.

'It's…positive.' Her voice sounded rusty. 'I'm… pregnant.' She handed him the test. He looked at it wordlessly and his jaw clenched. Clare swallowed. 'I can't believe it. Some couples try for months, years, even, to have a baby.' Her voice wobbled as the enormity of the situation hit her. She wished Diego would say something, give her some clue as to what he was thinking.

Diego walked over to the window and for a second he could not understand why he was surrounded by the sea, before he remembered that they were on board the super-yacht *Serendipity*. Memories of the DC Diamonds launch party flashed into his mind, but another memory—of the violent anger that had swept through him when he'd watched Clare dancing with her ex-boyfriend—tormented him.

Clare was expecting his child. The words ricocheted in his brain. Like his father before him, he had behaved with crass irresponsibility when he'd had unprotected sex, and the result was that Clare had conceived his baby.

He looked across the room at her sitting on the end of the bed. Her face was so white that the golden freckles on her cheeks and nose were starkly apparent.

'I assume from your silence that you are not pleased by the news,' she said flatly.

Diego turned his head away from her searching blue gaze. He had a feeling she could sense his panic, which made him want to run as fast and far away as he could. It occurred to him that he had been running away all his life.

'It makes no difference whether I am pleased or not. You are pregnant and it is my duty to support you and the child.' He could not bring himself to say *my child*, nor could he say he was pleased. His overriding feeling was of anger with himself, but he also realised that he must reassure Clare. 'I promise you won't have to deal with this alone.'

She went even paler, if that was possible. 'Deal with it? I'm not sure exactly what you mean by that but, make no mistake, I intend to go ahead with this pregnancy and have my baby.'

'Of course.' He stiffened when he realised she had

misunderstood him. 'It did not cross my mind that you wouldn't have the child.' The idea made him shudder, and he wondered if his mother had considered aborting him after his father had abandoned her when she was pregnant.

'Look…' He ran a hand through his hair and abruptly dropped his arm to his side when he saw her stare at his disfigured ear. He remembered the questions she had bombarded him with, which he had no intention of answering. 'We need to talk, but we both need some time to come to terms with what has happened. I'm due to give a press interview following last night's party. I suggest we meet back at the penthouse this evening for dinner and to discuss the future.'

Throughout the day Clare felt a sense of unreality. She went to her office, but there was little for her to do now that the PR campaign had finished. She had been expecting to book her flight back to England, but instead she was expecting Diego's baby. And until they had the discussion he had mentioned she had to remain in Brazil, not least because he still had her passport in his possession.

There was no reason for her to feel nervous, she told herself that evening when she stepped on to the balcony leading from the dining room. She and Diego had often had dinner alfresco over the past weeks and she was glad he had opted for them to eat informally tonight, sitting at the table with views of Copacabana beach.

Diego was standing looking at the view but turned his head when he heard her footsteps. He was wearing sun-bleached jeans that hugged his lean hips and a white T-shirt, through which Clare could see the delineation of his six-pack. Desire unfurled in the pit of her stomach and she avoided his gaze as she sat down on the chair he had pulled out for her. She shook her head as he was about to pour her a glass of sparkling white wine that she usually drank with dinner.

'I'll have water, thanks. I won't be able to drink wine for the next few months.'

'I'm sorry, I'd forgotten. Not about you being pregnant,' he said tersely when her brows rose. 'I guess we are both going to have to get used to a lot of changes, but you especially.'

She did not reply while the maid served dinner. Stew was a popular Brazilian dish, and the aroma given off by the casserole of white beans and sausage stirred Clare's taste buds. If she ate for two for the next eight months she would be the size of a house, she thought ruefully.

They ate in silence for a few minutes, before Diego opened the folder that was lying on the table and took out a document. 'I need you to sign some paperwork, specifically this form, which is to register our intent to marry.'

Clare's heart gave a jolt. She put down her fork and stared at him across the table. 'Marry?'

'Of course. It is the obvious thing to do.'

'It's not obvious to me.' Her appetite had disappeared. 'It's the twenty-first century and we do not have to get married because I'm pregnant.'

'My child will have my name,' he said in an uncompromising voice that matched the hard expression in his eyes. 'In reality, my child will have my mother's family name, Cazorra. I only discovered my father's surname was Hawke after his death. But he did not marry my mother and give me his name. I grew up wondering how a man could create a child but take no interest in his offspring. I won't allow the child we have created to feel compelled to search the faces of strangers, looking for some similarity of features and hoping to one day find the man whose blood runs through their veins.'

Clare swallowed the lump in her throat. Diego's poignant description of how he must have felt growing up without his father touched her deeply. *But marriage!*

She stood up and walked over to lean against the balcony rail. The sky was streaked pink and gold as the sun sank below the horizon. As dusk fell, the lights of the street lamps and from the skyscrapers that ringed the bay cast a silver gleam over the sea. Down on the ground the glow from car headlamps formed an unbroken line as traffic snaked along the main highway.

Rio was a vibrant, exciting city and Copacabana bay was undeniably beautiful, but Clare felt a long way from her home in a quiet north London suburb and from her family and friends.

'I understand how important it is to you that your child will know you as their father and bear your name. But expecting me to become your wife and live thousands of miles away from my parents is asking a lot.' Especially as he did not seem at all enthusiastic about marrying her. It was lucky she hadn't hoped for a romantic marriage proposal, Clare thought ruefully. Indeed, she had not considered marriage as an option. But if Diego were to take her in his arms and ask her to be his wife she would be tempted to say yes. And it was not only for the sake of their baby.

'I don't expect you to live in Brazil.' He stood up and came to join her at the railing, although she noted that he kept a distance between them. 'The marriage will be purely in the interests of the child. Being married will give us equal parental rights, and legally give my child my name, but I will agree to you and the baby living in England in a house that I will buy, and I will provide for you both financially.'

Clare gave him a puzzled look. 'Won't it be difficult to run the Cazorra Corporation and your various other businesses if you move to England?'

'I will continue to live in Brazil.'

The sharp pain beneath her breastbone was the sensation of her foolish dreams being torn to shreds.

'How do you propose to be a father if you are living on the opposite side of the world from your son or daughter?'

'I'll visit regularly, and often. The child will know that I...care about them,' Diego said tersely. Clare watched him curl his hand around the railing so that his knuckles whitened. She sensed he would rather be anywhere than here, having this discussion with her, but *too bad*, she thought grimly. They had both made this baby and she was furious that Diego seemed to think he could fulfil his responsibilities as a parent by throwing money at the problem.

'So your idea of being a good father is to turn up every couple of months, no doubt with an expensive present, take your kid to the zoo for an afternoon and then disappear again with a clear conscience?' She ignored his simmering look. 'Believe me, no amount of presents and occasional trips out could make your child believe you love them. I know because when I was a child, being taken to see a show once a year or being given the latest piece of technology did not reassure me that my parents loved me.'

Tears stung Clare's eyes as she imagined her child feeling the same sense of abandonment she had felt. Of course she would do her best to make up for the fact that Diego would be a mainly absent father, just as Aunt Edith had tried to be a substitute parent. But in her opinion a child needed both its parents, and Diego's idea of good parenting fell far short of ideal.

* * *

The condemnation in Clare's voice scraped Diego's conscience raw, and he spun away from her and strode into the penthouse to evade the accusation in her sapphire-blue eyes. Ever since the helicopter had brought them back to the Cazorra skyscraper, he had debated with himself what would be best for his child.

He grimaced as he acknowledged the bitter truth that the best way he could protect his child was to send them to live as far away from him as possible. All afternoon, while he'd given a series of press interviews about the DC Diamonds launch, his mind had flashed back to when he had watched Clare dancing with her ex-boyfriend at the party. His searing, jealous rage that had made him want to smash his fist into Mark Penry's handsome face.

He did not know what he was capable of if he lost his temper and he did not want to look into the darkness of his soul to find out. Since he had been released from prison he had avoided situations that might make him angry. He had perfected a persona of a laid-back, imperturbable playboy so successfully that he had started to believe it. But last night his jealous reaction to seeing Clare with Penry had shattered his illusions about himself and proved that although he had suppressed his emotions for nearly twenty years he had not eliminated them.

'Do you have a better suggestion?' he demanded as Clare followed him into the lounge.

'As a matter of fact, I do.'

Diego noticed her gaze dart to his rucksack and old leather hat that he'd left by the door, and he saw a question forming on her lips. He folded his arms across his chest. 'So, what is it?' he drawled.

'I suggest that we get married for real. You want to give your child your name, but what a child needs most is a sense of belonging and of knowing that they are loved unconditionally, ideally by growing up with both their parents. That isn't always possible for some people, but why don't we at least try to make a go of marriage for our baby's sake? Instead of being a part-time parent, why not be the father you wished your father had been when he left you to grow up in a slum?'

Emotions he had fought against for so long flooded through Diego. It was as if a tidal wave inside him had burst through the barricades he had painstakingly built. He hated himself when he saw a flash of hurt in Clare's eyes as he shook his head in a silent negative answer. He realised how much it must have cost her to ask if they could have a proper marriage. She was proud, but she had sacrificed her pride for what she believed would be the best for their child, and Diego admired her even more than when she had risked her life to rescue her sister.

But he couldn't do what she had asked. He could not take the risk. What if they argued and he lost his temper with Clare? What if, God forbid, he lost his temper with his child? The thought filled him with icy fear. The only way he could ensure their safety was to live away from them, and when he visited England he would make sure he was never alone with his child.

'You know my feelings about marriage.' He managed to strike his usual tone of sardonic amusement. He swung his rucksack over his shoulder and jammed his hat on his head, pulling the brim low over his eyes. 'I don't share your idealised belief that the only thing a child needs is love. Try telling that to the thousands of children who live in extreme poverty and don't even have the basic requirements of food and shelter, let alone access to education that would help them escape the *favelas*.'

He walked over to the door and glanced back at Clare. Was it his imagination or did her breasts look slightly fuller beneath the cream silk dress she was wearing? Her auburn hair tumbled in silky waves around her shoulders. *Deus*, would he ever escape the spell she had cast on him that made him think of her all the time, and want to be with her day and night?

'I will provide you and the child with an excellent standard of living. You will want for nothing. There will be no need for you to work, unless you choose to resume your career at some point.' He hesitated. 'I realise that you are young and attractive and might want to have a personal relationship…with a man,' he elaborated when Clare looked puzzled.

'Are you suggesting I could have an affair?'

'As long as you were discreet for the child's sake.'

The idea of Clare with a lover caused bile to burn like acid in Diego's throat and he gripped the door handle as he fought the temptation to stride across the room and pull her into his arms.

'Are you *leaving*?'

He heard disbelief in her voice and could not bring himself to look at her. 'I have to fly up to Boa Vista to carry out a geological survey of a potential gold mine site in the rainforest. Before I go I'll submit our registration of marriage form. We are legally required to give twenty days' notice prior to getting married. We will marry when I return to Rio, and after the ceremony I will arrange for you to fly back to England.'

'Go then.' Clare gave a contemptuous laugh. 'Run away, Diego. When you helped Becky and me to escape from Rigo and his henchmen I believed you were the bravest man I'd ever met. But I see now that you are a coward. It makes no difference how much money or material possessions you give to our child, because if you won't even try to be a proper father you are no better than the man who fathered and abandoned you.'

Her words stabbed Diego through his heart. Clare was right; he *was* no better than his father. But it was not cowardice that had led to his decision to live apart from his child. Clare did not understand that he was trying to protect their baby and her.

He groaned and slumped against the door. 'I *can't* be the husband you want me to be, or the kind of father I wished for when I was a boy,' he said harshly. 'There are things about me that you don't know.'

'So tell me.' Her voice was no longer contemptuous, but soft and clear as a mountain stream, and the scent of roses filled Diego's senses when she walked over to him and placed her hand lightly on his shoulder. 'Help me to understand your demons, because the child we created so carelessly will need both of us to be part of their life.'

Diego turned round and stared down at her. She was so petite next to his tall frame, so fragile compared to his muscular build. The knowledge that he could easily hurt her terrified him. He was certain that if he told her the truth about himself she would insist on taking their child to live far away from him, away from the danger he represented. But where did he start? He remembered the questions she had asked that morning when she had woken him from his nightmare.

'You had better sit down,' he said roughly. When she did so, he sat on the sofa opposite her and took off his hat, twisting the brim between his fingers.

'I met Miguel in prison. We shared a cell—' he grimaced as memories of the terrible conditions flooded his mind '—along with ten other prisoners.' He looked up and saw Clare's startled expression. 'We were both on remand. Miguel had been accused, wrongly, of fraud, and I was waiting to be tried…for murder.'

She drew a sharp breath. 'Were you wrongly accused like Miguel? Or…had you actually…killed someone?'

'I don't know.' Diego looked away from the horror he could see in Clare's eyes. 'I don't remember.'

'I don't understand.' Clare's voice shook as she tried to absorb Diego's astounding revelation. 'How can you not remember whether you murdered a person? Surely it's not something you'd forget.'

Diego saw her place her hand on her stomach, as if she was instinctively seeking to protect the fragile new life developing inside her. Protect their child from him, he thought grimly. But, strangely, now that he'd started to talk he wanted to continue. He couldn't run away from himself any more, he acknowledged, feeling a bone-aching weariness from twenty years of running and hiding from his past. Clare was clearly shocked, but she was still here, waiting for him to explain.

'My mother was a drug addict,' he said emotionlessly. 'Dealers often used our one room in the tenement as a base where they sold drugs, and most nights I slept on the streets and searched for food in bins.'

Clare pictured Diego as a little boy, roaming the dark and dangerous alleyways of a slum, searching for a place to shelter for the night. Learning that she was pregnant made his description of his childhood even more poignant.

'By the time I was a teenager I'd seen things no child should see, and from necessity I'd learned how to take care of myself. I was hot-tempered and often involved in fights.' Diego twisted his hat in his hands. 'One night it was raining hard and I had nowhere to go but home. When I arrived, I found my mother bleeding and crying while her dealer beat her because she could not pay for her next fix.'

He swallowed convulsively. 'She was only little, about the same height as you, and defenceless.' He took a deep breath. 'I lost my temper and punched the guy. Hard. I wanted to kill him.'

'But did you?' Clare said shakily.

'I honestly don't know. The guy retaliated and we fought. The last I remember was his fist coming towards my face. The next thing I knew was when I opened my eyes and saw the man lying on the floor and a pool of blood round his head.' Diego's voice was hoarse. 'It was obvious he was dead. The police had arrived and my mother told them…' He fell silent.

'What did your mother tell the police?' Clare prompted.

'She said I'd gone crazy and kept punching the guy even after he'd collapsed to the floor. According to my mother, I had been in a manic rage and she had been unable to stop me from hitting the man. It was as if I had suffered some kind of fit that made me act with uncontrolled violence, until eventually I passed out.'

Diego forced himself to look at Clare. She was obviously shocked by what he had told her but, to his surprise, there was no hint of revulsion in her blue eyes.

'The police arrested me and charged me with murder,' he continued. 'At seventeen I should have been sent to a juvenile detention centre, but it was full so I was locked up in an adult prison to await trial. But I couldn't afford a lawyer and the only witness to what had happened was my mother, who had disappeared.'

'You must have been scared. How long were you held in prison?'

'Two hellish years. It's where I lost the top of my ear.' He brushed his hair back to reveal his disfigured ear. 'I saved Miguel from a beating by some of the other prisoners, and as punishment they held me down and sliced off part of my ear with a razor blade.'

'Dear God,' Clare whispered. 'No wonder you have nightmares.'

'I was befriended by the prison chaplain, Father Vincenzi.' Diego's strained features softened into a smile. 'The priest is a truly good man. He believed I was innocent and fought to have the charges against me dropped due to a lack of evidence.'

Diego recalled the mixed emotions he had felt on the day he had walked out of prison: relief that he was free, but also a terrible uncertainty that perhaps he was guilty of murder, which he still felt two decades later.

'After I was released I went to stay with Cruz and his family and we both worked in Earl Bancroft's diamond mine. A few years later, Father Vincenzi was contacted by a lawyer in England who was trying to find me to give me the news that I was the heir of the lawyer's deceased client, a man called Geoffrey Hawke. He was my grandfather and he'd left me a sizeable fortune in his will, which enabled me to buy the Old Betsy diamond mine with Cruz.'

'Why did the priest believe you were innocent?' Clare asked.

'There were inconsistencies in the statement my mother gave to the police. Also, forensic evidence indicated that the man had died from a blow to the back of his head by something heavy. But I have no recollection of using a weapon. Father Vincenzi thought that my mother may have lied about what actually happened.' Diego shook his head. 'But she knew I would go to prison. Why would my own mother lie to the police about me?'

'I don't know.' Clare frowned. 'Have you ever tried to find her to ask her?'

'I searched for my mother for years and I believe she is still alive, simply because if she were dead her death would have been registered. A couple of times there were promising leads, and a year ago I received information that she was being treated in a hospital. But I had no response when I tried to contact her and since then she has disappeared again. I came to the conclusion that she doesn't want to see me, and I stopped looking for her.'

'Why wouldn't she want to see her only son,' Clare

mused, 'unless she has something to hide? It suggests
that she *might* have lied to the police.'

Diego rubbed his hand across his brow. 'It suggests to me that my mother witnessed me turn into
a violent murderer and she is scared to meet me,'
he said grimly. 'Don't you see, Clare? *I don't know
if I lost my temper and killed a man.* Perhaps I was
gripped by a manic rage, as my mother said, and I
can't take the risk of it happening again in front of
my child. *I dare not be a proper father when there
is a chance I am a murderer.*'

He dropped his hand down from his face, and
Clare's heart turned over when she saw a betraying
glimmer of moisture in his eyes. She thought of how
he had protected her in the rainforest and helped her
to rescue her sister from the kidnappers. Feeling an
instinctive need to comfort him, she got up from the
sofa and knelt in front of him.

'Diego, you were a boy of seventeen, and you were
trying to protect your mother from being beaten,' she
said gently. 'Even if you did punch the man who was
hitting your mother, it wasn't a premeditated attack.
I don't believe you would have intended to kill him,
and I don't think a judge would have believed it either. Father Vincenzi obviously didn't believe you
were a murderer, or he wouldn't have worked to secure your release from prison.'

He looked unconvinced, and his jaw clenched. 'I
won't risk our child's safety, or yours, when I don't
know if I can trust myself to control my temper.' His

throat worked as he swallowed hard. 'Last night I had proof that I still have a hot temper. When I saw you dancing with Penry, I wanted to throw him over the side of the yacht and I hoped he'd drown.'

Clare's eyes widened. 'Why did you feel like that?'

'I was jealous,' Diego grated. 'It's not an emotion I am familiar with,' he added, sounding more like his old, cynical self.

He had been jealous because she'd danced with Mark! Clare forced her mind back to Diego's harrowing story of his past. 'You might have wanted to throw Mark overboard, but you *didn't* act on those feelings, which shows that you can trust yourself to control your temper.'

His hand was resting on his knee, and she linked her fingers with his. 'You don't know if you were unwittingly responsible for a man's death, but I *do* know that you saved my life and my sister's life when you arranged our escape from Rigo. I'm sorry I accused you of being a coward,' she said in a choked voice. 'It must have taken a lot of courage to tell me the reason why you feel you can't be a proper father.'

She looked into his eyes. 'In Torrente you asked me to trust you, and I am ashamed that at the time I didn't. But I do now. I trust you completely, and I want to help. It seems to me that the only way for you to come to terms with your past and move forwards with your life is if you make another attempt to find your mother and discover the truth about what really happened when you were seventeen.'

Diego looked down at their linked fingers and felt

as if his heart was being squeezed in a vice. Clare was as fierce as a tigress and he was touched by her determination to help him. But her faith in him and her refusal to judge him strengthened his resolve to protect her and their child from himself if necessary.

'If I find my mother, are you prepared to learn the truth about me, whatever it might be?'

She held his gaze steadily. 'Nothing your mother might say will make me lose my trust in you.'

CHAPTER ELEVEN

HOSPITALS ALWAYS SMELLED of disinfectant, Clare thought as she walked with Diego into a hospice in the city of Belo Horizonte. She recalled the private hospital in Rio, where a week ago she and Diego had had an appointment at the antenatal unit for her ultrasound scan. The scan had confirmed that she was now twelve weeks pregnant.

She had been surprised at how clear the image of the baby was when the sonographer had pointed out on the screen the infant's head and chest and a tiny beating heart. Tears had filled Clare's eyes at this first sight of the child developing inside her, and when she had glanced at Diego and had seen his jaw clench she knew he was trying to hide his emotions.

Since his revelation that he might have killed a man twenty years ago, they had both been living in a strange sort of limbo. Clare had insisted that they wait until she was safely past the three-month stage of her pregnancy before they discussed marriage. She had suffered badly from morning sickness, and the constant nausea plus the pregnancy hormones zooming around her body had made her desperately tired so that she was often in bed by early evening.

She had felt quite relieved that Diego hadn't suggested they resume a sexual relationship. Her wan complexion and the fact that she had to rush to the bathroom all the time was probably not a turn-on for him, she thought ruefully. But, with sex off the agenda, a different relationship had developed between them and they had become good friends. To Clare's surprise, Diego talked openly about his deprived childhood and the terrible two years he had spent in prison, and speaking about his horrifying experiences seemed to be cathartic for him.

He had asked Clare to work on ideas for a publicity campaign to raise money for the Future Bright Foundation, and she had been glad of something to do to take her mind off feeling sick. The charity project was also the reason she had given her father to explain why she could not return to England and resume her role as head of A-Star PR. She had decided not to tell her parents about her pregnancy until she had some idea of what would happen between her and Diego. Rory Marchant had sounded happier than he had for a long time as he'd explained that her mother's health had improved significantly and he was now able to go back to running the agency.

Another surprise had been the news that Brazil's most wanted criminal, Rodrigo Hernandez, known as Rigo, had been arrested for drug trafficking. A few days ago the Estrela Rosa, the Rose Star Diamond, had been returned to Diego. But Clare knew he was not thinking of the diamond as they walked through the hospice where, he had learned two days ago, his mother was a patient.

He had hired a team of private detectives to search for his mother but, as the weeks had gone by, Clare had secretly begun to despair that Shayla Cazorra would ever be found, and Diego would never discover what had really happened when he had been a teenager. Whatever had taken place that night twenty years ago would not alter her belief that Diego had been a victim of circumstance, a boy who had been trying to protect his mother. She trusted the man who had protected her since she had come to Brazil, and she could no longer deny to herself that she loved him.

She pulled her mind back to the present as a nurse stepped out of a room and greeted them. 'Your mother is awake, Mr Cazorra, and she is anxious to see you.'

Clare gave his arm a gentle squeeze. 'I'll go and sit in the waiting room while you talk to your mother.'

'I'd like you to meet her.' His jaw was rigid. 'I intend to tell her about the baby and this is perhaps the only chance for her to see you.' He glanced at the nurse, who gave a nod of confirmation.

'Your mother's cancer is very advanced and I am sorry to have to tell you that she does not have long to live.'

They went into the room. The woman lying in

the bed was desperately thin and her dark hair was
streaked with grey. Clare could see no resemblance
between her and Diego, but Shayla Cazorra held out
her bony hand to her son, who she had not seen for
two decades.

'Diego, *meu filho. Me perdoe*,' she whispered.

'*Mãe.*' Diego did not know how he had expected
to feel when he met his mother after so many years.
He had thought of her so often, especially while he
was in prison, and he'd felt angry that she had disappeared when he'd needed her. But hearing her call
him *my son* evoked an ache in his chest. He would
not have recognised the husk of a woman who looked
so frail lying on the pillows. Instinctively he knew
she had days rather than weeks to live.

'*Mãe*, this is Clare.' He spoke in Portuguese,
guessing that his mother had not learned to speak
English since he'd last seen her. 'We are going to
have a baby.'

Shayla's face crumpled. '*Me perdoe*,' she said again,
tears sliding down her cheeks.

Diego could feel his heart thudding beneath his
ribs. '*Me perdoe* means *forgive me*,' he translated
quietly for Clare. He took his mother's hand in his
and felt her bones beneath her papery skin. 'Why do
you want me to forgive you?' he asked her gently.

Instead of replying, she lifted up her other hand
from the bed and gave him a piece of paper which
he saw was a handwritten letter. For a moment he
hesitated, afraid to read it. Would he finally learn

the truth about himself? He felt sick. What if his mother's letter confirmed that he had killed a man years ago? A small hand slipped into his and he glanced at Clare and thought, as he often did, that he could drown in her deep blue eyes.

'I think your mother wants you to read the letter,' she urged softly.

Taking a deep breath, Diego skimmed the words his mother had written, once, twice. *'Deus...'* His voice was choked with emotion.

'What does it say?' Clare asked tautly.

'She killed him.' He read the letter a third time. 'While I was fighting with the man I'd found beating my mother, she hit him on the back of his head with a chair leg. She realised he was dead. I was unconscious from the punch he'd landed on me just before she attacked him. Someone had called the police, and she panicked and told them I had killed the guy while I'd been in a manic rage.' He exhaled heavily. 'She explains in the letter that she thought I would be sent to a youth detention centre, but she knew she would spend the rest of her life in prison and she was scared of being locked up in a cell.'

Diego's throat ached and he felt an unfamiliar sting of tears in his eyes. For twenty years he had been haunted by the idea that he could be a murderer, and all the time he had been innocent. Tears were sliding down his mother's face and his gut clenched. She hadn't been much of a mother, but she hadn't had much of a life after his father had seduced her and abandoned her when she fell pregnant, Diego thought. He looked into his heart and found no anger, just pity.

'*Mãe...*' He took a tissue from the bedside cabinet and wiped away her tears. '*Eu perdoô voce.*' *I forgive you.*

He did not see Clare wipe tears from her eyes as she quietly left the room.

The flight from Belo Horizonte back to Rio took an hour, and it was late afternoon when the limousine that had collected them from the airport drew up outside the Cazorra skyscraper. 'Are you sure you didn't want to stay at the hospice with your mother?' Clare asked as they walked across the foyer.

Diego shook his head. 'We both said everything we needed to say.' His mother had fallen asleep while he'd sat with her, and the nurse had assured him that Shayla was sleeping peacefully for the first time since she had been admitted to the hospice.

'You don't have to come in the lift with me,' Clare said as he followed her into the elevator. 'I know you prefer to take the stairs.'

The lift door closed and Diego waited to feel the familiar tightness in his chest, the sensation that he couldn't breathe. But nothing happened. He could breathe normally. He thought of the time Clare had helped him cope with his claustrophobia by kissing him. Her distraction method had certainly worked, and the memory of the passion that had blazed between them had a predictable effect on his body.

They had not made love for over two months while she had been suffering with sickness caused by her pregnancy. He had felt guilty that it was his fault she was so pale and fragile, but in the last few days the nausea had lessened and now she looked radiant. There was colour in her cheeks again and her auburn hair shone like silk. To anyone else her pregnancy was not yet visible, but Diego noted that her breasts were fuller and there was a new voluptuousness to her body that made him long to undress her and explore her lush curves.

'How do you feel?' she asked innocently.

Deus, he wasn't going to admit he was so turned on by his fantasies of having sex with her that he was surprised she did not notice the bulge of his erection beneath his trousers.

'You must feel relieved now your mother has told you the truth, that you didn't kill a man.'

'I'm still stunned,' Diego admitted. 'For twenty years I was afraid that I was capable of extreme violence, and I avoided close relationships because I didn't trust myself. Now it's as though a huge weight has been lifted off me and I feel free.' Life suddenly seemed full of possibilities and for the first time in his life he was excited by the future, Diego realised.

As he looked at Clare, he was aware of a strange constriction in his chest that was not caused by his claustrophobia. His gaze lowered to the very faint

swell of her stomach and the ache in his heart intensified as he visualised the scan image of their baby
that he had seen on the ultrasound screen a week ago.

Emotions flooded through him, but he had spent
twenty years suppressing his emotions and he was almost afraid of the strength of his feelings. He needed
to regain control of himself and take charge of the
future.

'We need to talk, and make plans,' he said gruffly.
'First off, you need to sign the document so that we
can register our intent to marry.' He frowned as the
lift halted unexpectedly at the eighth floor, which
was where the Cazorra Corporation's offices were.
The doors opened and a huge cheer went up from
the dozens of members of staff who were crowded
around the lift entrance.

'What's going on?' Diego demanded as his PA
stepped forwards.

'The figures for DC Diamonds' first two months
of trading have been issued, and profits are double
what they were predicted to be,' Juliana explained.
'I'm sure you haven't forgotten that you had arranged
for all the staff to be paid a bonus today. Everyone
wanted to say thank you.' She had to raise her voice
above the loud cheer that went up from the crowd.

Diego glanced at the sheet of figures Juliana had
given him and grinned. 'The profits made by the
Cazorra Corporation's newest venture are certainly
something to celebrate with champagne.'

The staff gave another cheer, someone was blowing into a *vuvuzela*—a long plastic trumpet more usually heard at football matches. Champagne corks shot into the air and Diego was pulled into the party.

Clare was left alone in the lift. She watched Diego chatting with Juliana before he was mobbed by some of the dancers from his nightclub, who crowded round him. The sound of his laughter was audible above the babble of voices and he looked more relaxed and happier than Clare had ever seen him. But moments ago he had been frowning when he'd mentioned the marriage application document, which she had yet to sign.

She pressed a button to close the doors, and as the lift ascended to the top floor she pictured Diego surrounded by his staff who clearly adored him. He had looked as if a weight really had been lifted from him. For the first time since he had been freed from prison he was truly free.

Diego sipped his champagne and looked around the open-plan office for Clare. He smiled as he watched his staff enjoying the impromptu party, but he could not see her auburn hair amid the crowd, and when he asked his PA if she'd seen her, Juliana shook her head.

He wanted to celebrate DC Diamonds' success with her. After all, it was Clare's brilliant PR campaign to promote the jewellery shop that was responsible for the excellent profits. He owed her so much. Without her support he would not have made another attempt to find his mother and he would have spent the rest of his life believing he had once acted with such violence that he had killed a man.

He understood now that he had deliberately avoided close relationships because he had been afraid of hurting someone he cared about if he ever lost his temper. But now that fear had gone, just as his irrational fear of confined spaces had disappeared. When he had told Clare he felt free, he hadn't fully realised the implications of his new-found freedom. He did now. He was free to admit to the emotions surging through him, free to open his heart to love.

The lift took him swiftly up to the penthouse and he checked in the lounge and library before he hurried down the hallway to Clare's bedroom. His heart was pounding with a mixture of nerves and hopeful anticipation, but when he knocked on the door and entered her room he felt a jolt of surprise that turned to unease as he saw her rucksack on the bed.

She walked through from her sitting room and Diego's confusion deepened at the sight of her in the khaki shorts and T-shirt that she had been wearing when they had escaped from Torrente. His gaze zoomed to her passport that she was holding and he guessed from her pink-rimmed eyes that she had been crying. That shocked him the most. He had never seen her cry before, even when she had been scared by the python in the rainforest and terrified by the far more dangerous snake Rigo.

He wanted to stride across the room and pull her into his arms, but two decades of hiding his feelings was a hard habit to break, and he leaned nonchalantly against the door frame and folded his arms over his chest. 'I see you found your passport in my room, although I don't know why you need it. I'm also curious about why you are wearing your old clothes. Are we going to take another trip through the rainforest? I'll get my hat.'

She walked over to the bed and dropped her passport into her bag, taking care, Diego noted, to avoid looking directly at him. '*We* are not going anywhere,' she said flatly. 'I've decided to fly home to England. I don't want to tell my parents about the baby over the phone.'

'Fine, we'll go together so that I can meet your family before we get married. We can even have our wedding in England if you want.'

'I don't. I…I'm not going to marry you.'

'*Deus*, Clare.' Diego's iron grip on his emotions snapped. 'What the hell is the matter? You agreed we would get married once you had passed the first three months of your pregnancy.' He strode over to her and caught hold of her shoulder, spinning her round to face him. She was pale, and the sight of faint tear streaks on her cheeks made his gut clench. 'Do you feel ill? I thought the sickness was getting better.'

'I feel fine.' She dropped her head but Diego slid his hand beneath her chin and tilted her face upwards. She was so beautiful. He breathed in the fragrant rose perfume she always wore and felt a flare of panic when he realised how tense she was. Was she afraid of him?

'You know that my mother admitted she killed the guy, not me,' he said hoarsely. He remembered his mother had written her confession in Portuguese. 'If you don't believe me, I'll give you the letter and you can have it translated.'

'I do believe you.'

He wasn't convinced. 'You have nothing to fear from me, *querida*. I would never hurt you or our child.'

'I know you wouldn't.' Clare bit her lip. This was even more difficult than she had expected. But she knew she was doing the right thing, and her resolve hardened. 'We don't have to be married for our baby to take your name. When he or she is born we can simply register them with the name Cazorra. Nor do we have to be married to be parents to our child. I am willing to move to Brazil so that we can live near each other and take an equal share of parenting. Many families have arrangements that aren't conventional, and if we both try we can make the arrangement I've described work for us and, more importantly, for our child.'

A cold hand of fear curled around Diego's heart when he saw Clare's determined expression. 'When we first found out about your pregnancy, I told you I couldn't be a proper husband and father because I was afraid that I might be a murderer and I could not put you or our child at risk of my temper. But now I know the truth and I am free of that worry.'

'Exactly,' Clare said huskily. 'You are finally free, Diego. You spent two years in prison but twenty years imprisoned in your mind for a crime you didn't commit. Do you think I haven't worked out that you shunned relationships and never allowed yourself to fall in love because you were afraid of yourself, and afraid that you might be a manic killer? That must have been an unbearable burden to carry.'

She had to be brave, even though she could feel her heart breaking, Clare told herself. 'I conceived your baby as a result of a moment of madness. I refuse to sentence you to be imprisoned in a marriage of convenience because you feel it is your duty to your child. For the first time in your life you are free to fall in love and choose the woman you want to spend the rest of your life with.'

Wild and uncontrollable emotions were storming through Diego, smashing down the last of his barriers and making him feel exposed and vulnerable in a way he had never felt before. He thought he understood what Clare was doing, why she seemed to be pushing him away. But he could be wrong and if he was, and she really did not want to marry him, then the future looked unbearably bleak.

'And what if I choose you as the woman I want to spend my life with?' he said roughly. 'What if I told you I love you? Would you agree to marry me then?'

She shook her head and Diego stared into the abyss.

'It's a little too convenient for you to suddenly decide you are in love with me.' There was a catch in her voice. 'I know why you said it. I know you want to be a devoted father like you wish your father had been. I promise I will never come between you and your child.' A single tear slipped down her cheek and she hastily wiped it away. 'You will be a wonderful father,' she choked out, but Diego did not appear to be listening.

'*Convenient!* There is nothing convenient about loving you, *anjinho*. I knew when I first saw you, a picture of innocence in your nun's habit and veil, that you were trouble,' he growled. 'I wanted to do all sorts of unholy things to you, and when we made love in the cave I was willing to pay for my sin of desiring you by spending the rest of my life in purgatory—because that night was the most beautiful night of my life.'

He cradled her face in his hands and gently wiped another tear from her cheek with his thumb. 'I should have been furious when I discovered you had tricked me and were not committed to a life of religious devotion, but all I could think of was that you were free to come to my bed.' His eyes darkened with remembered shadows. 'But I wasn't free to follow my heart and fall in love with you. I had to protect you from the monster I believed was inside me.'

'Oh, Diego, it breaks my heart to think of all the years you spent alone, fearing to love anyone,' Clare whispered.

He breathed deeply and prayed for the first time in his life. 'The truth is that I never met any woman who touched my heart until I met you, *meu amor.*' His voice deepened. 'I love you, Clare. Not because it is convenient and not because you are carrying my child. I love you because you are the bravest, craziest, most beautiful, sexiest woman I have ever met. When you told me you trusted me, you made me feel like I could conquer the world. But I don't want the world, all I want is you. Our baby will be a wonderful bonus. But I am asking you, *querida,* I am begging you to marry me, because you are everything to me and without you I am nothing.'

The look in Diego's eyes was love, Clare realised dazedly. His words had chipped away at her defences, but the raw emotion blazing in his silver gaze made her believe him.

'When I said I wouldn't marry you, I was trying to be noble,' she explained shakily. 'You could have any woman you choose…'

'I choose you,' he said fiercely. 'I don't want you to be noble, I want you to love me.'

She heard the boy beneath the man, the poet who had read words of love but never heard them spoken to him. Clare reached up and stroked her fingers across the blond stubble on his jaw, traced his beautiful mouth with her fingertips.

'I do love you, with all my heart and all my soul. You are the other half of me, my hero, my protector, my lover and my husband—I hope,' she added tremulously.

'Try and stop me,' Diego whispered against her lips, before he claimed her mouth and kissed her with all the passion and tenderness and love that he had kept locked inside him for so long, until Clare had unlocked his heart and set him free.

Six months later baby Rose Cazorra entered the world and promptly stole her parents' hearts.

'You wouldn't believe such a tiny baby could have such a loud cry,' Diego said as he cradled his daughter in his arms. 'I think Rose has inherited your fiery temperament, as well as your red hair and blue eyes,' he told Clare.

She smiled. 'You could be right. Mum says I had a very loud cry when I was a baby. I can't wait for my parents to arrive tomorrow to visit their new granddaughter. We haven't seen them since our wedding.'

They had married in England five months earlier in a simple but intensely moving ceremony at Clare's parish church. She had worn a white dress decorated with tiny crystals, and white rosebuds in her hair. Diego had looked eye-catchingly handsome in a light grey suit, but his eyes had been focused on his new wife as they had stood on the steps of the church and he'd swept her into his arms and kissed her.

'Te adoro,' he had whispered to her on their wedding day, and he repeated those words now, first to his baby daughter as he placed her in her crib, and

then to Clare when he lay down beside her on their bed and drew her into his arms. 'You are my world, you and Rose, and I will take care of you and protect you and love you every day of my life,' he vowed.

'Only every day?' She pretended to pout. 'Will you love me every night, too? Starting with tonight.'

Diego felt his body stir as desire heated his blood when Clare tugged the straps of her negligee down and her breasts spilled into his hands. 'It's only a few weeks since you gave birth to Rose. Do you feel ready for me to make love to you, *querida*?'

'I always want you to love me,' she whispered, tugging him down on top of her.

'I always will, *anjinho*.'

* * * * *

In case you missed it, book one in the
BOUGHT BY THE BRAZILIAN *duet*
MISTRESS OF HER REVENGE
is available now!

Uncover the wealthy Di Sione family's
sensational secrets in the brand new
eight book series
THE BILLIONAIRE'S LEGACY *beginning with*
DI SIONE'S INNOCENT CONQUEST
by Carol Marinelli
Also available this month.

Turn the page for an exclusive extract of
SLEEPLESS IN MANHATTAN,
the first book in USA TODAY *bestselling author*
Sarah Morgan's enthralling new trilogy,
FROM MANHATTAN WITH LOVE!

PAIGE STOOD FOR a moment, thinking how unpredictable life was.

Who would have thought that herself, Eva and Frankie losing their jobs would have turned out so well?

Urban Genie existed only because life had laid a twist in her path.

Change had been forced on her, but it had proved to be a good thing.

Instead of fighting it, she should embrace it.

What had Jake said?

Sometimes you have to let life happen.

Maybe she should try to do that a bit more.

And maybe one day she'd look back and realize that *not* being with Jake was the best thing that could have happened—because if she'd been with Jake she wouldn't have met—

Who?

Would she ever meet someone who made her feel the way Jake did?

She stood leaning on the railing, gazing at the city she loved.

The lights of Manhattan sparkled like a thousand stars against a midnight sky and now, finally, as the last of the guests made their way to the elevators, she allowed herself a moment to enjoy it.

"Time to relax and celebrate, I think."

Jake's voice came from behind her and she turned to find him holding two glasses of champagne. He handed her one. "To Urban Genie."

"I don't drink while I'm working." And while Jake was present this was definitely still work.

She knew better than to lower her guard a second time.

"The guests have gone. You're no longer working. Your job is done."

"I'm not off duty until the clear-up has finished." And then tomorrow would be the follow-up, the post-mortem. Discussions on what they might have done differently. They'd unpick every part of the event and put it back together again. By the time they'd finished they'd have found every weak spot and strengthened it.

"I don't think one glass of champagne is going to impair your ability to supervise that. Congratulations." He tapped his glass against hers. "Spectacular. Any new business leads?"

"Plenty. First up is a baby shower next week. Not much time to prepare, but it's a good event."

He winced. "A baby shower is *good*?"

"Yes. Partly because the woman throwing it for her pregnant colleague is CEO of a fashion importer. But all business is good."

"Chase Adams is impressed. By tomorrow word will have got around that Urban Genie is the best event concierge company in Manhattan. Prepare to be busy."

"I'm prepared."

His praise warmed her. Her heart lifted.

He stood next to her and the brush of his sleeve against her bare arm made her shiver.

His gaze collided briefly with hers and she thought she saw a blaze of heat, but then he looked away and she did, too, her face burning.

She was doing it again. Imagining things.

And it had to stop.

It had to stop right now.

No more embarrassing herself. No more embarrassing *him*.

She turned her head to look at him but he was staring straight ahead, his handsome face blank of expression.

"Thank you," she said.

"For what?"

"For asking us to do this. For giving us free rein and no budget. For trusting us. For inviting influential people and decision-makers. For making Urban Genie happen." She realized how much she owed him. "I hate accepting help—"

"I know, but that isn't what happened here. You did it yourself, Paige."

"But I wouldn't have been able to do it without you. I'm grateful. If you hadn't suggested it, pushed me that night on the terrace, I wouldn't have done it." She breathed in. Now was as good a time as any to say everything that needed to be said. And if she said it aloud maybe it would help both of them. "There's something else—" She saw him tense and felt a flash of guilt that he felt the need to be defensive around her. *Definitely* time to clear the air. "I owe you an apology."

"For what?"

"For misreading the situation the other night. For making things awkward between us. I was…" She hesitated, trying to find the right words. "I guess you could say I was doing an Eva. I was looking for things that weren't there. I was close to panic and you were trying to distract me. I understand that now. I don't want you feeling that you have to avoid me, or be careful around me. I'd never want that. I—"

"Don't. Don't apologize."

He gripped the railing and she noticed his knuckles were white.

"I wanted to clear it up, that's all. It was a kiss. Didn't mean anything. Two people trapped in an elevator, one of whom was feeling vulnerable." *Shut up right now, Paige.* "I know I'm not your type. I know you don't have those feelings. I'm like your little sister. I get that. So—"

"Oh, for— *Seriously?*" He interrupted her with a low growl and finally turned to face her. "After what happened the other night you really think I see you as *a little sister*? You think I could kiss you that way if I felt like that about you?"

She stared at him, her heart drumming a rhythm against her chest. "I thought— You said— I thought you saw me that way."

"Yeah, well, I tried." He gave a humorless laugh and drained his champagne in one mouthful. "God knows, I tried. I've done everything short of asking Matt for a baby photo of you and sticking that to my wall. Nothing works. And do you know why? Because I *do* have feelings, you're *not* little and you're not my damn *sister.*"

Shock struck her like a bolt of lightning.

They were the only two people left on the terrace. Just them and the Manhattan night. The buildings rose around them—dark shapes enveloping them in intimate shadows and the shimmer of light.

The storm clouds were gathering, creating ominous shadows in the dark sky.

The sudden lick of wind held the promise of rain.

Paige was oblivious. The sky might have come crashing down and she wouldn't have noticed.

Her mouth was so dry she could hardly form the words. "But if you feel that way, if you do have feelings, why do you keep saying—" She stumbled over the words, confused. "Why haven't you ever done anything about it?"

"Why do you think?"

There was a cynical, bitter edge to Jake's tone that didn't fit the nature of their conversation. None of the pieces fitted. She couldn't think. Everything about her had ceased to function.

"Because of Matt?"

"Partly. He'd kick my butt. And I wouldn't blame him." He stared down at his hands, as if they were something that didn't belong to him. As if he was worried about what they might do.

"Because you're not interested in relationships—or 'complications' as you call them?"

"Exactly."

"But sex doesn't have to be a relationship. It can just be sex. You said so yourself."

"Not with you."

His tone was harsh and she took a step back, shocked. They'd often argued, baited each other, but she'd never heard that edge of steel in his voice before.

"Why? What's different about me?"

"I'm not going to screw you and walk away, Paige. That's not going to happen."

"Because of our friendship? Because you're worried it would be awkward?"

"Yeah, that, too."

"Too? What else?" She stared at him, bemused. He was silent.

"Jake? What else?"

He swore under his breath. "Because I care about

you. I don't want to hurt you. There's already been enough damage to your heart. You don't need more."

The first raindrops started to fall.

Paige was still oblivious.

Her head spun with questions. *Where? What? Why? How much?* "So you— Wait—" She struggled to make sense of it. "You're saying that you've been *protecting* me? No. That can't be true. You're the only one who *doesn't* protect me. When everyone else is wrapping me in cotton wool, you handle me as though you're throwing the first pitch at a game."

He didn't protect her. He *didn't*. Not Jake.

She waited for him to agree with her, to confirm that he didn't protect her.

He was silent.

There was a throbbing in her head. She lifted her fingers to her forehead and rubbed. The storm was closing in—she could feel it. And not just in the sky above her.

"I *know* you don't protect me." She tried to focus, tried to examine the information and shook her head. "Just the other night, when we found out we'd lost our jobs, Matt was sympathetic but you were brutal. I was ready to cry, but you made me so *angry* and—" She stared at him, understanding. She felt the color drain from her face. "You did it on purpose. You made me angry on purpose."

"You get more done when you're angry," he said flatly. "And you needed to get things done."

No denial.

He'd goaded her. Galvanized her into action.

"You challenge every idea I have." She felt dizzy. "We fight. All the time. If I say something is black, you say it's white."

He stood in silence, not bothering to deny it, and she shook her head in disbelief.

"You *make* me angry. You do that on purpose. Because if I'm angry with you, then I'm not—" She'd been blind. She breathed hard, adjusting to this new picture of their relationship. The first boom of thunder split the air but she ignored it. "How long? How long, Jake?"

"How long, what?" He yanked at his bow tie with impatient fingers.

His gaze shifted from hers. He looked like a man who wanted to be anywhere but with her.

"How long have you cared? How long have you been p-protecting me?" She stumbled over the word—and the thought.

He ran his hand over his jaw. "Since I walked through the door of that damn hospital room and saw you sitting on the bed in your Snoopy T-shirt, with that enormous smile on your face. You were so brave. The most frightened brave person I'd ever seen. And you tried so hard not to let anyone see it. I have *always* protected you, Paige. Except for the other night, when I let my guard down."

But he'd been protecting her then, too. He'd been taking care of her when she'd been so terrified she hadn't known what to do.

"So you thought I was brave, but not strong? Not strong enough to cope alone without protection? I don't understand. I thought you weren't interested, that you didn't want this, and now I discover—" It was a struggle to process it. "So this whole time you *did* care about me. You *do*."

Rain was falling steadily now, landing in droplets on his jacket and her hair.

"Paige—"

"The kiss the other night—"

"Was a mistake."

"But it was real. It wasn't because I was a pair of red lips in an elevator. All these days, months, *years* I've been telling myself you didn't feel anything. All the time I've been confused because my instincts were so wrong and I couldn't understand why. But now I do. They weren't wrong. *I* wasn't wrong."

"Maybe you weren't."

"So why let me think that?"

"Because it was easier."

"Easier than what? Telling me the truth? News flash—and, by the way, I thought you knew this— I don't want to be protected. I want to live my life. You're the one who's always telling me to take more risks."

"Yeah, well, that proves you shouldn't listen to anything I tell you. We should go inside before you catch pneumonia."

He eased away from the railings and she caught his arm.

"I'll go inside when I decide to go inside." The rain was soaking her skin. "What happens now?"

"Nothing. I know you don't want to be protected but that's tough, Paige, because that's what I'm doing. I'm not what you're looking for and I never have been. We don't want the same thing. There's a car waiting downstairs to take you and the other two home. Make sure you use it."

Without giving her a chance to respond, Jake strode away from her toward the bank of elevators and left her standing there, alone in the glittering cityscape, watching the entire shape of her life change. Another twist. Another turn. The unexpected.

Don't miss SLEEPLESS IN MANHATTAN
by Sarah Morgan, available from HQN Books.

#3453 MARRYING HER ROYAL ENEMY
Kingdoms & Crowns
by Jennifer Hayward
Most women would kill to be draped in ivory and walking up the aisle toward King Kostas Laskos. But Stella Constantinides naively bared her heart to Kostas to disastrous effect once before and this feisty princess refuses to be his pawn ever again.

#3454 HIS MISTRESS FOR A WEEK
by Melanie Milburne
Years ago, Clementine Scott clashed spectacularly with arrogant architect Alistair Hawthorne and swore she'd never have anything to do with him again! But when Clem's brother disappears with Alistair's stepsister, she's forced to go with Alastair to Monte Carlo to retrieve them!

#3455 IN THE SHEIKH'S SERVICE
by Susan Stephens
Sheikh Shazim Al Q'Aqabi must resist his instant attraction to mysterious dancer Isla Sinclair, for duty is Shazim's only mistress. Until Isla is revealed as the prize winner who will travel to the desert to work with him...making their chemistry impossible to ignore.

#3456 CLAIMING HIS WEDDING NIGHT
by Louise Fuller
Addie Farrell's marriage to casino magnate Malachi King lasted exactly one day, until she discovered their love was a sham. Now Addie must prepare to face her husband—and their dangerously seductive chemistry—once again!

EXCLUSIVE
Limited Time Offer

$1.00 OFF

USA TODAY BESTSELLING AUTHOR
SARAH MORGAN

Sleepless in Manhattan

FREE BONUS STORY

"A LITTLE SWEET AND A LOT SEXY."

$7.99 U.S./$9.99 CAN.

USA TODAY Bestselling Author
SARAH MORGAN

introduces From Manhattan with Love,
*a sparkling new trilogy about three best friends
embracing life—and love—in New York.*

*Paige Walker loves a challenge, but can she
convince a man who trusts no one to take a
chance on forever?*

Sleepless in Manhattan

*Available May 31, 2016.
Pick up your copy today!*

HQN

- ✂

SPECIAL EXCERPT FROM

HARLEQUIN

Presents

A Harlequin Presents® brand-new eight-book series,
The Billionaire's Legacy: *the search for truth and the
promise of passion continues…*

*Charity CEO Allegra Di Sione can't fail in her mission
to retrieve her grandfather's beloved box from Sheikh
Rahim Al-Hadi—which is why she gets caught in
Rahim's sumptuous bedroom trying to steal it!*

Read on for a sneak preview of
THE DI SIONE SECRET BABY

"I came here to set a few things straight with you," Rahim
sneered, deeply resentful that she'd led him to question
himself when there was no doubt where his destiny lay.
"You thought what happened in Dar-Aman wouldn't go
unchallenged. You were wrong."

Allegra's hand jerked to her stomach, her eyes more
vivid against her ashen colour. "No. Please…"

From across the room, Rahim saw her sway. With a
curse, he charged forward and caught her as her legs gave
way. It occurred to him then that she hadn't answered him
when he'd asked what ailed her. Swinging her up into his
arms, he carried her to the sofa and laid her down.

With a low moan, she tried to get up. Rahim stayed her
with a firm hand. "I'm going to get you some water. Then
you'll tell me what's wrong with you. And what the hell
you're doing giving long speeches and photo ops when
you should be in bed."